# Treats
# & Tales

Treats & Tales
Copyright © 2022 by Rotha J. Dawkins

Published in the United States of America
ISBN    Paperback:      978-1-959165-41-5
ISBN    eBook:          978-1-959165-42-2

All rights reserved. No part of this publication may be reproduced, stored in a retrieval system or transmitted in any way by any means, electronic, mechanical, photocopy, recording or otherwise without the prior permission of the author except as provided by USA copyright law.

The opinions expressed by the author are not necessarily those of ReadersMagnet, LLC.

ReadersMagnet, LLC
10620 Treena Street, Suite 230 | San Diego, California, 92131 USA
1.619. 354. 2643 | www.readersmagnet.com

Book design copyright © 2022 by ReadersMagnet, LLC. All rights reserved.

Cover design by Ericka Obando
Interior design by Daniel Lopez

# Treats & Tales

Rotha J. Dawkins

# TABLE OF CONTENTS

PART I
NOVEL: *LIL' RED & FRIENDS* ...............................1

PART II
TREATS: RECIPES FOR CANINES.................................166
GOOD MANNERS FOR DOGS..........................................178
SHORT STORY: *"CANDY"*......................................180

PART III
TREATS: DRESSING YOUR DOG...................................196
(HOW TO MAKE DOG CLOTHES)

# Dedication

To my grandchildren:

Isaac, Grace, and Cana Hunt

It's always fun playing together, especially with our animals. This book is for you!

My love to you always,
Grandmother (Rotha)

# Acknowledgements

Thank you for the following people that helped me in getting this booked published.

Ericka Obando - Cover Designer
Daniel Lopez - Interior Designer
Rob Gonzales - Publishing Production Supervisor
Bob Marquez - Publishing Consultant
Lu Vasquez - Author Relations Supervisor
Red Sanchez - Author Relations Officer

# Part I

Lil' Red and Friends
Novel
Rotha J. Dawkins

"Peppermint Dawkins"
Age 4

When you acquire your dog or cat, it's a real moment. That bonding is like love at first sight.

Peppermint was in the Davidson Country Animal Shelter. Probably, she had been bounced around and not treated well prior. She was too thin and a bit frightened. It was only days before she came around as though she had always been mine.

To have a baby like her is not to be "lonely," someone "there" and never to "talk to yourself" anymore.

There is a special "void" that animals replace. The love, attention, frolic, and play is worth it all. No words can ever say how we feel. I guess it's simply magic!

I love you Peppermint!
"Mother Rotha"

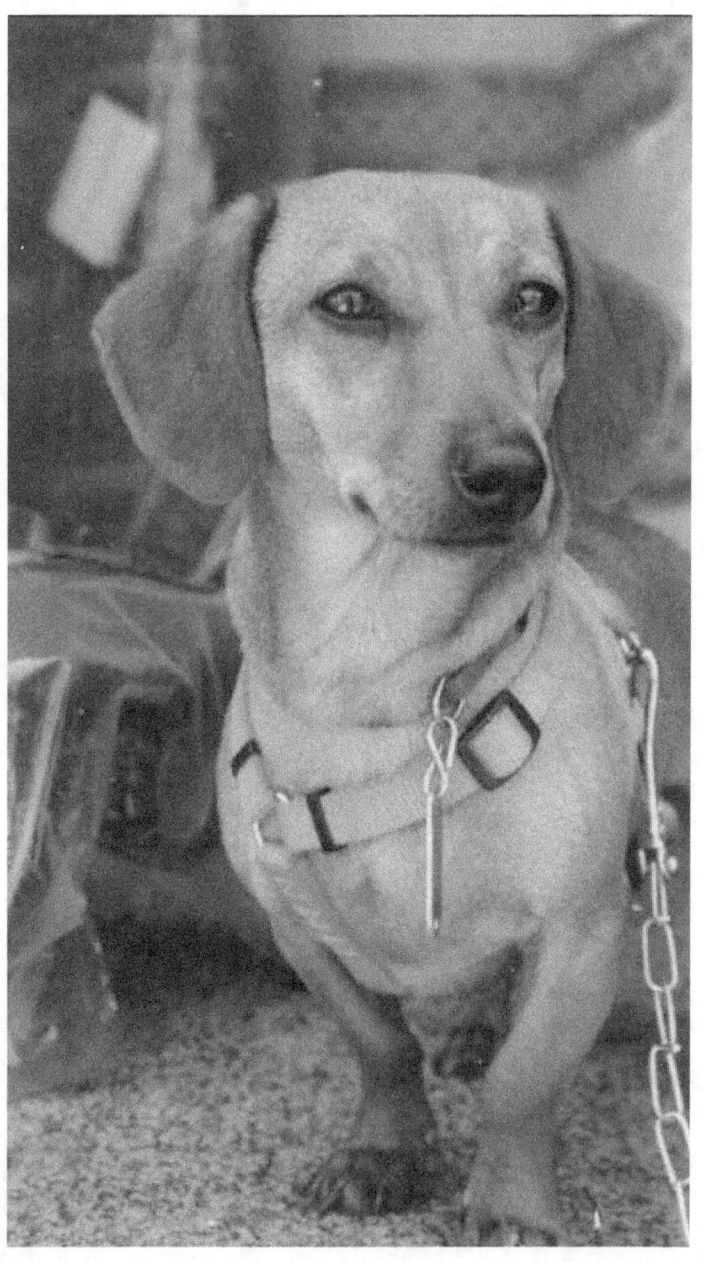

# Chapter 1

"Get in there!" screamed the helper. He reached down to unsnap the leash on the red dachshund who was holding back, and sliding. She gulped and gritted her teeth. Opening the big door to a space full of other dogs, he slung her all the way inside. As she soared in the distance, her ears flew outward as did all four legs as if in flight.

The landing wasn't comfortable when she plopped onto the head of a huge pit-bull that quickly flipped her off. He growled, gobbling at her with his mouth and shook the little body bringing blood with pain.

The helper then hit a cage with a stick. The Sunnydale Animal Shelter was jammed full of creatures. There was literally no more space.

The left entry hallway consisted of cages with assorted puppies and dogs. For most of these varied animals: Being born was a mistake.

In the wide aisle that smelled like a combination of 'Pine Sol' and smeared 'po-do' people could scrutinize the animals. A little girl screamed, "Oh look, it's a 'weenie' dog!" She started singing, "I'd like to be an Oscar Mayer Wiener!"

The red dog dropped to the floor, remarking to a tail-wagging white French Poodle, "Did you hear that? She's calling me an Oscar Mayer Wiener! I hate that! Besides, that's a Jewish name. I'm German American."

"Well, look at the options; go with the kid or stay here. In three days, you'll burn. They'll put you to sleep," answered the poodle. "I'm showing off for her! Watch this!"

Quickly, the white dog dropped to the floor and rolled. The little girl exclaimed, "Let's get that cute curly dog. Please!"

As fast as you can say scat to a cat, the iron doors of the cage-room slid open. A uniformed arm snatched up the pretty white dog and placed her in the arms of the child.

Poodle looked at Red sadly, "It's been nice knowing ya Red Dog. You'd better cop a better attitude or you're gonna smoke! Hope you'll each find a home!"

Red Dog walked to a German Shepherd. "Hey big dog!"

The shepherd grunted, "Hey. Me and Terrier here are trying to get a grip on things."

"It ain't great here but it's better than last week," Terry said. "An old woman picked me up behind a shopping center. I sort of lived there while I was homeless. I hate being homeless, especially in the winter. She didn't like me though. I don't mean to be so nuts, but when you have to whiz, you gotta 'go'. I did it in her kitchen floor; guess it teed her off, so here I am!"

"I chomped a mail man. Actually, I barely nipped him. He'd kick me for no reason when coming through the fence. I'll be here until the quarantine is over. My ole man got real mad about 'Sue' somebody," the shepherd moaned.

"Sue? Oh yeah, humans hate that word. It means somebody will take their stuff if they can. You can't bite 'em; just scare them to death!" Red smiled then settled onto the cement.

Red was happy the pretty poodle bonded with the new family. 'Poodles are curly and French fashionable. They never have to take ridicule. They are accepted for the fluffy, uppity, eccentric creatures they are. Give them a bow in their hair, then watch that nose stick in the air,' thought Red. 'Fluffy would be a good name for her.'

Another dog was slipped into the cage. Looking at her Red could see the stomach sagging almost to the ground with her sides extra wide. The dog plopped to the floor and sighed, "See they dumped me! I'm going to have puppies. This will be my first time. You know what, I'm just eight months old myself."

"Gee, that's too bad. Didn't you know about the puppy thing?"

"Well, I do now! Ouch! One just kicked me in the belly!" She grunted, "What's going to happen to us?"

"You're a beagle, people like you because you can hunt rabbits and stuff." Red sniffed her long hanging ears.

"I suppose," sighed the black and tan.

"I've got an idea. If we stay in this dog pound three days, we'll be dead. We've got to find a way out of here! They try to pretend we'll get adopted and cared for but that's not always true. There's too many dogs and not enough homes," snapped Little Red dogmatically.

The big German Shepherd overheard. "You've got the right idea. We have to do something. Look over here. See where that bucket of water sits? It's dirt! Tonight we can dig under this wall and leave this jungle."

"I'm afraid!" squeaked a mix-breed Collie, Dalmatian and Shepherd.

"Don't be stupid! Just keep yourself quiet and help," growled the Shepherd.

"But we might get caught!" She shook. Her whole body was nearly vibrating.

"Dumb ox! So? What can happen if we are found out? Die; that's the plan if we don't escape," yelled Little Red. "I wish I could fly. Oh how I wish I could fly! Sometimes I think I can!"

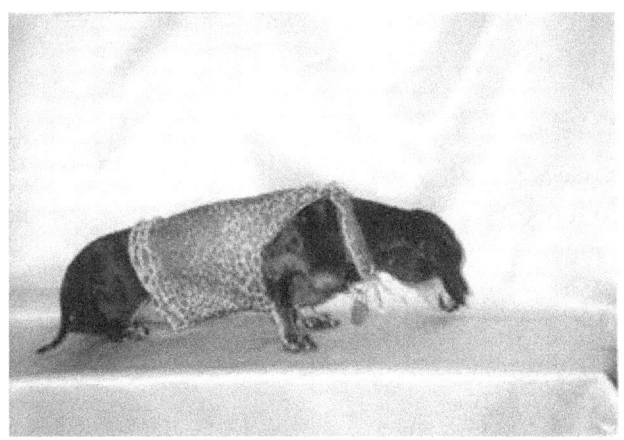

# Chapter 2

"Dogs don't fly! Never! Dogs don't fly!" laughed the Beagle. She flipped her long brown ears.

"We will all fly when we get out of here. This place is on a real high hill. I'll show you!" whispered Little Red. "Sh! Here comes old grouch with our food. Play possum!"

"Possum?" winced Beagle. "Yes, act like you're asleep — that's what possums do!" Red quickly rolled on her side and shut her eyes.

The fellow opened the door and poured a bag of dry food into a huge container. He snickered to himself. "Look at these lazy ugly devils. Ain't got nothing going for 'em but sleep. Come Friday, you'll all go to the state lab. They'll use you like rats, then burn you. Too bad you were ever born." He touched the fat belly of the Beagle. "Poor little girl. Maybe I'll take you home to my grandpa. He likes hunting dogs. You'll be able to have eight or ten more litters of pups. At three hundred dollars a puppy and about six of them at a time, you can make some money for us."

None of the dogs moved. Finally, he walked out the door and down the long hallway. The day was almost over. Someone began turning lights off; only the dim rays from the fleeting sun and a few night-lights remained. Soon vehicles outside the building were driven away in other directions. Everything became quiet.

A dog outside the building began to whimper with a scared cry. Those inside the various rooms keenly listened.

Red stood, "It's the Poodle! Mercy what happened to her?"

Finally the doggy cried out, "Red?" Ohhh! Red Dog?"

"Hush! We're in here!" replied Red. We hear you."

"I want to come back!" I'd rather die than be with that mean little brat!" wept the Poodle. "Help me in!"

"Are you crazy? We're coming out! All of us!"

"That's right!" snorted 'Mark' the Shepherd. "How did you get back here?"

"Didn't get far at all. Those people put me in their car with that girl. She smacked me around, pulled my hair, and even spit in my face. Can you imagine how humiliated I felt?"

"*Milliated*? Is that like rich? Millionaire you mean!" whispered Beagle.

The Poodle adjusted the new pink collar. "No, oh no. *Humiliated* means the most horrible of feeling awful, like spit-dirty and nasty. I should be so lucky to be rich. I'd rather die in this gas chamber than be with a terrible person like that."

"It's good you're back. We're breaking out of here tonight," informed Red. We must be real quiet. You can keep watch out for us."

"This will be hard to do," complained the mixed breed just beside Red.

"But we'll do it! We can start digging in here, in fact, right in front of Fluffy on this side of the wall," Red promised.

"I have never dug anything in my life," breathed the Poodle. Tell me how and I'll dig out here."

"Great idea!" praised Little Red. "Just stretch your front feet before you and scratch at the ground. Do one paw at a time. As you get good at it, go faster. Try it!"

Little Red began digging inside creating an indention. It was tiring work; she began to pant. Being small and long seemed easy. Still the short legs could only open the passage the size of her tiny head making it quite tight on her shoulders. Finally, she backed out revealing red dirt on her black nose and paws.

The dogs standing around laughed. "I look funny but I'll bet that white Poodle is a sight!" smiled Little Red. She called out, "Poodle? Are you alright?"

The fluffy dog stopped to answer, "Whee! This is fun! I love it!"

The Dalmatian giggled, "Fluffy, how far have you dug?"

"I can crawl all the way into this hole! Hot dog, this is super!" squealed Fluffy, and then groaned. "There's something real hard here! Oh no, what will we do?"

From the inside Little Red discovered the same wall. She backed out of her neatly dug tunnel. "We have to figure this out. It can't be the end. Maybe it's a wall."

"That's a footing. They pour them to keep us from digging," Dally said. "When I was at the fire department I watched them dig a trench for that building. It is supposed to give a building support."

"You're so smart Dally," whispered Beagle.

He looked at her wide stomach and laughed. "Looks like I may have to take care of you girl. Wait until these long legs start digging. I can already see those little short sawed-off devils aren't going to make a dent for my big lard fanny!"

Dally stuck his long arm into the deep hole. He teased the Dachshund, "Sugar Pie, you're about like a tiny drill bit making a starter hole. Let me show you what digging really is. What's this?"

Dally felt something on the left side of the hole. He wiggled his paw and felt deeper, then rejoiced. "Oh! Marvelous! I'm touching Fluffy ... That's the Poodle's hand!"

From outside they heard an excited voice. "You found me! You found me! I'll keep digging!" Thrilled, Fluffy kept a digging frenzy.

# Chapter 3

Dalmatian widened the hole inside to open the space large enough for everyone to follow. He'd dig to the left, then to the right and all through the middle. Dirt was flying everywhere, then came a portion of small rock. Soon, he sat down with his tongue hanging out, "Whessh! That's tough digging! I need to rest. Hey Collie, come on over and help!"

Suddenly, a *whine* and an *oomph*, then a little head snapped up in the hole. Poodle had made it back inside. She grinned from ear to ear, "Bet no dog ever broke into the pound!"

All the dogs gathered around sniffing and squawking their approval.

Collie ambled to the newfound passage, "That's only big enough for little dogs; we have a lot more digging to do. Step aside Miss Fluffy!"

Fluffy said, "No, I'll go back outside and dig more." She darted out followed by a Rat-Terrier mix, Little Red and a Chihuahua. Once under the wall they began to dig together in a row beside the first hole to widen the passage.

Collie urged, "Great dogs, absolutely great dogs! Dig wide and deep!"

"You got it!" giggled Fluffy. "I just love this!"

The three outside kept their pace in unison, looking like an extra wide roto-tiller. "We're getting there!" puffed the Chihuahua named Peppie. "We're getting under the wall!"

The Collie inside felt Peppie's paw and screamed, "I touched a hand! I know I did!"

"Right on! It's mine," exclaimed Peppie. "It's mine!"

They shook hands in the dirt then both continued with the others helping. They were letting the dirt fly as if they were searching for gold.

Suddenly, there was a big noise from in back of the building. They heard heavy footsteps moving toward them.

Little Red jumped, "People are coming! We have to hide this quick! Peppie, you, Terry, and Fluffy stay out there. If I bark three times run! Otherwise, stay close."

"Alright," agreed Peppie.

Red pulled herself out of the hold. "Hurry Dal, Collie and you Big Thing! Lay over this hole! Hide our diggings!"

The three flopped into the space and covered the loose dirt and hole. Lil' Red smiled, "You'll pass inspection except the dirt on your head and paws. Dally, clean your face; be quick!"

The big Dalmatian rushed to the water bucket and ducked his head totally under water.

Beagle sniffed, "Oh no! Dal is killing himself!"

About that time, Dally pulled his from the water and stuck his front feet inside the huge pail and shook, "How do I look?"

"Great! Hurry over there! I hear the people!" explained the Dachshund. "Here they come! Play asleep!"

Every dog stretched into a sleep position.

An interior door rattled, people stepped inside. A man spoke, "Mayor, we are so crowded. We have to send our overflow to 'market' weekly."

Something has to be done about the large amount of strays. Sit down a minute," he said. "Sunnydale can't handle this."

Little Red understood, "They're talking about us!"

"I've got to potty," whispered a young dog.

"Good!" laughed Collie, "Hey, everyone let's potty!"

"Good idea!" snickered a Bulldog. "Do it beside the door!"

"Shish! Do it quietly!" giggled Red. In the dim light, they each did their part next to the big entrance door. Rushing back to their sleep positions, each dog settled down with satisfaction.

Again the voices became louder from outside the bars. A heavy fist pounded a desk. A voice screamed, "Who needs a bunch of nasty strays? The city has enough problems. I don't have time to spend with the 'animal rescue' stuff. It's simple, get rid of the devils that are costing the taxpayers' money!"

The Mayor spoke cautiously, "Mr. Small, I understand your thoughts but keep in mind its taxpayers that put these little creatures here. There needs to be a responsible program enforced. If we don't do something, we'll never gain on this problem."

"He's right!" insisted another man. "These animals aren't at fault. We are!"

"We don't have enough money to feed, house, and care for the bunch of useless critters," argued a man. "I vote to let the medical research lab have everyone we can get.

Pick them all up and send them out right away. They'll pay twenty dollars a stray dog and ten for each cat."

"I suppose we can take a vote tomorrow when we have a quorum," sighed the Mayor.

"Election is right around the corner," reminded the man. "This should be income, not outgo money."

"I just believe there has to be a better way," the Mayor added. "People still need to be forced to take a responsible stand. Being sorry never is a solution."

Another man said, "Let's take a look in the big kennel."

Chairs scraped, then people were walking toward the kennel.

"They're coming!" whispered Red. "Get ready!"

All the animals stretched into a comfortable position. Soon, seven people were at the door of their space.

A woman grabbed her nose, "My goodness! This is horrible. It stinks worse than the septic plant! Whes-sh!"

"I thought you people kept this place clean!" screamed the Mayor.

"Want to go inside and look at the animals?" asked the pound attendant.

"I'm not walking in that!" screamed the woman. "This is inhumane!"

The group turned and the lights were turned off. They muttered all the way out the building. Once gone, the dogs laughed, turned flips and rolled.

"Great idea! We stunk them out!" Beagle giggled.

# Chapter 4

"You heard it; they'll send us to the med-lab. That's where we are used for research," reported Lil' Red sadly. "I'd rather just be burned here than that!"

Beagle sniffed, "We have to do something fast. Oh! Oh! Stop kicking! Oh! Wow, that was hard pain."

"Are your puppies telling you something?" whispered the big Dalmatian.

"Oh yes! I think they want to be born soon!"

"Just hold on! Please hold on! We've got to get out of here. Don't let them be born now!" pleaded Dally.

"I'll lay here," whimpered Beagle. She looked real fat in the middle. When she plopped to the floor her eyes closed and a mass of water suddenly gushed over the cement around her.

"Get to digging! Beagle is going to give birth right now! Look at her! She is so beautiful. Dally make them dig it wider and deeper. I've got to help our beautiful mommie!"

The others put their efforts to taking turns digging while Dally and Lil' Red observed Beagle.

Lil' Red directed, "Dally, bring me that towel over there. We need to put it under her."

He did as told.

"Stretch the towel flat. Now lift her feet," ordered Red. Dally moved Beagle into place with his mouth.

Beagle was panting hard then she began to moan in beagle howl, "Oh-hoh-ho! Oh-hoh-ho!"

Lil' Red smiled, "Lay on your side. Push your back to the wall. People say it's easier if you count then breathe."

"I know! I'll try," wailed Beagle. "How do I do it?" Then she again cried with pain, "Oh! Ohh-h-ho!"

"Sh! Sh! Sh!" comforted Red. "Now, breathe! In… out… in… out! Blow it! Three times!"

Beagle took a breath and blew out… "One!" smiled Red. "Again! Two, breath in, now out… three. Again. Now push if you're ready!"

Beagle followed Red's direction. Over and over again for a very long time. She was tired and looked at her friends with tears, "My babies won't come out! They should but something is wrong. Oh Red, help me."

Dally sat up, "Red, she's getting weak. Look at her!"

Red stared at her friend who was in pain with birth. "Alright, we've got to do it now! Collie, when we count to three she's going to breathe then push. You press gently high and downward. I'm going to reach for a baby."

"You need some boiling water?" snorted a big Lab.

"Bring us any kind of water!" replied Collie.

"Alright Beagle come on! Take a deep breath! Good! Good! Now out! Two… breathe in! Good girl, yes now out! Come on, honey, three take it in; now, let it out and push! Push! Push hard!"

The little fat beagle did push hard and Red saw a little foot come to the surface. "Keep on Beagle, we have a puppy; here I have it! Oh it's a boy look! He's beautiful!" Suddenly, they rescued the puppy covered with a mass of satin-like material and a long funny-like tail.

"Oh, God she's had a snake!" observed a Lab.

"No, that's the umbilical cord. That was feeding tube when he was inside," answered Dally. I'll cut the cord, but the mother always cleans the baby.

Red mauled at the squeaking tiny life that she placed before the mother dog. "Are you alright?"

"Oh yes, but I'll be ready again soon." She hurriedly cleaned the puppy and chewed the cord to a short length. She smiled, "I'm ready, Red my mid-wife!"

Again they did a three-time breath count and once more Red helped pull the wet baby outside at the same time another foot appeared and number three puppy slipped out head first.

"We have two more! Oh this is special!" screamed Lil' Red. "Beagle you have three now! Oh my goodness! Take these I've got to get your next puppy; I see him coming!"

While Red carefully worked to bring the baby to life, Beagle gave a big push then continued her chore of removing the membranes from around the puppies. As number four was complete, Beagle whispered, "I'm not done yet Red. Here comes another one."

Again, another baby slipped into the world. With another push the after-birth cleared the birth canal. Beagle looked at Red and smiled, "Thank you, let me finish here. I have to clean house and feed my puppies. Five great babies!"

"Let's give her some privacy 'Dr. Red'," smiled Dally. "Looks like I'm an adopted Father. Wish I had some cigars!"

The two went to the "digging job." Collie had directed his group to make the exit easy. A three feet wide and over two feet deep spot was complete. The dogs took time drinking water then huddled around Lil' Red.

Collie panted, "It's done. You could get a human through here."

"Well, we need to get ready to go. Once the hole is discovered, they'll pour cement in that too. You can bet they don't want to lose their prisoners," said Red.

"Let's take all the food we have here," suggested a miniature dachshund named Zipper.

"That won't work. We have to run once we get out. Remember, this is a run for your life," a very thin greyhound insisted. "When I used to race, I was not given a lot of extra food. What we should do is eat enough to get by. Let the little dogs have first dibs. Y'all get over there and eat for the road. Just listen to the plan."

Zipper took the lead and began crunching the dry mix. Fluffy, Peppie, and the other little ones joined him. They sounded like a little popcorn machine. Soon, Zipper stepped back, "That's enough for now. We'd better not drink too much. This stuff swells up in your belly."

The larger dogs gathered around and ate about a cup of food each.

# Treats & Tales

# Chapter 5

"Beagle! Can you eat?" whispered Dally. "We have to go."

"Not now. I just finished that mess with the puppies." She smiled and lifted her head. "I'm so tired. I can't go on."

"We will not leave you. I told you that I would look after you. You come along or we won't go!" he replied. "We will find a way."

"That's right!" agreed Red, Zipper, Fluffy, Collie, and the others in unison. "You and the babies are going!"

"I'll try," whispered Beagle. She felt weak. The pups were stretched in a row pumping milk from her breast.

"We'll be fine once we get away from here. We'll run a couple miles. It's late so we can use the roads some." Lil' Red planned.

"What about the police? We can't let them see us as a pack," Zipper injected.

"I know it," replied Red. "If we see moving lights, we can jump in the grass or behind the trees and bushes then law low. Anyhow, there's so many of us they'll never catch us!"

"Yup! The circus is in town. They'll think we're leopards, tigers, wolves, coyotes, and such!" grinned Peppie.

"Yeah, they might think I'm an elephant!" boasted a big Saint Bernard. He grabbed a piece of black water hose that had been used as a whip. Hooking it between his teeth, he flipped it around and gave a strange shrieking grunt.

They all laughed.

"We must get with it. Five of us can carry a puppy and somebody has to help Beagle. Ain't your name Bonnie Girl?" asked the big German Shepherd named Mark.

The black and tan dog smiled, "Yes, that's it. Why is your name Mark?"

"Cause I used to mark the territory when I lived at summer camp. I just stayed there as a bum in a way. That *marking job* kept the raccoons, deer, and critters away. Snakes don't like "wee-wee" either!" Mark boasted. "That was real talent! I earned my keep."

"When we get outside, we've gotta split! It's late now; I can't hear traffic. Let's get the babies first," Red suggested. "Beagle, are you ready? Do you feel alright?"

Bonnie was standing over her little puppies. "Maybe I should stay here. I'm sorry; I feel weak."

"I know you can't feel good just having those little things, but tomorrow you'll be dead for sure if you stay here in the Nazi camp," growled Dally. "You get out that hole over there and leave the rest to us."

"Dally is right! We all go together. We'll find a way." Lil' Red promised.

Quickly, they helped Bonnie out; then, everyone else took their turn getting through the tunnel. Each expressing happiness to being outside.

"Sh! Sh! Sh! We have to be quiet. Let's rest a few minutes," Peppie whispered. "This air tastes good!"

"It's wonderful," agreed Bonnie. "I feel better already."

"Alright, be real careful carrying those puppies. Don't drop them either!" cautioned Lil' Red. "I'll carry one, Peppie you can do this too. Who else wants a puppy?"

Dal said, "Give me one of my sons!"

"Shep and Mark can take the other two," smiled the mother dog.

With that settled, they had to decide who would help Bonnie. She was shaky from the ordeal of birth.

"I'm used to running," insisted the Greyhound.

"Yeah, but you're too skinny. It would be like riding a pile of bones," snorted the Great Dane. "I'm tough. When I lay down, put her on my back."

"You might be tough, but I'm wide and fat. That pretty little momma is going to be my guest. She'll feel like she's floating on a fluffy blimp!" snickered Bernie the Bernard. "Bring that big long towel out here."

The Lab happily retrieved the long rag. "Here!"

The huge cushiony dog gently positioned himself on the ground. "Bonnie, get on my back and put your front legs around my neck; dig in with your back ones. Now, don't I feel good?"

"Oh my yes! You're like the softest feather bed in the whole world. This was worth having pups!" she laughed.

"Great! I'm your ambulance, we can't make Dally jealous," Bernie teased. "Dal, throw that long cloth over her and put the ends in my mouth," ordered the Saint Bernard.

He wrapped it over and pulled the ends in front of Bernie then carefully pushed it toward the giant dog's wide-open mouth. Quickly, Dal jumped back. "Oh mercy!"

"What?" grinned Bernie.

"That huge mouth and set of teeth looks like a short alligator. Suppose you'd drop that jaw too soon; I'd lose a hand!" he laughed.

"Alright, let's go!" Lil' Red ordered.

"Wait a minute! You and Peppie are too little to haul these two babies. Besides, you two can run ahead. Red, you have to lead the pack. Let me take one and give the other puppy to Spike," grinned the thin greyhound as she pointed to a mixed breed with an ear erect and the other flopped half way over the right side of his head.

"That will be perfect. You mean you trust me with a baby?" Spike questioned Babe, the sleek beautiful retired greyhound.

# Chapter 6

Lil' Red, Peppie, Zipper, and Fluffy set out in front of the rest of the pack. It was the perfect time of night to roam. It didn't take them very long to stretch the first couple of miles. At that point, they became tired and winded.

"We need to stop. Look! There's a beautiful water fountain. We can drink water here," panted Peppie.

"Alright, that will work, but we have to be real quiet," Lil' Red agreed. "Be silent and don't move around much."

"I need to feed my babies," reminded Bonnie. "My chest is burning from this milk."

The huge Saint Bernard gently eased to the ground. Bonnie slipped off his back and rolled over and under a bush. The puppies were put beside her. With very little help, they quickly claimed their personal tit and nature took its course. Being so newborn, it didn't take them long to eat.

"I'll *puppy-sit* for you," smiled Lil' Red. "They are so cute. You get some water and rest."

"Thank you," whispered Bonnie. She then started toward the pool. Dalmatian caught up to her on the dark side of the fountain. They leaned on each other as they squatted to lap water.

"Let me give you a bath," Dally suggested.

"That sounds good; I need one. I feel so unclean. It's a dirty job having puppies," laughed Bonnie and slipped deliberately into the pool. She stood in the water. "Wow! This is cold but it's wonderful."

Dally followed her in then laid down in the splashing water. The fountain surged its spray continually.

It didn't take long until all of the other dogs joined in the comfort of a community bath.

"Stay quiet!" warned Lil' Red, still watching the puppies. They lay in a pile together. "I want to bathe too. But you enjoy yourself Bonnie. The babies are fine."

Soon, the dogs began to wrestle and play in the fantastic large fountain. In the distance, they heard a police car whine toward their direction.

"Oh no! We're caught!" cried Fluffy as she jumped from the water and rolled in the grass to dry.

"Don't freak out! Stay still and shut up!" ordered Red. "Get out of the water and ease into the bushes."

A black and white car with flashing lights stopped at the sidewalk where the seven steps lead to the bubbling fountain. The streaks from the blue and pink spotlights enhanced the beauty of the solitude. The policeman slammed his car door and walked directly to the beautifully man-made lagoon.

The pack of dogs lay quietly in the surrounding bushes. Their refuge was filled with leaves, spider webs and debris. They could see every move of the cop. Each animal was frightfully trembling. They knew if discovered, it would be the end. They watched.

"Anyone in here?" called the cop. He used a very long black flashlight to pour extra light for search. "Come on out!"

The man waited, then walked to the edge of the ever-flowing fountain. He looked inside the water. As he turned to leave, he muttered, "Streakers… bums… kids! Always one or the other. I expect big bubbles will flow by morning."

He was remembering other calls to the city square. Once, somebody had emptied a box of wash soap. Bubbles were all over town. Another time, somebody emptied a bottle of red dye and it looked like there had been a mass murder. Then, there was the time when three dozen kids from a college were being inducted into their fraternity. They wore nothing.

He shuffled to open his car door. A radio inside was talking. The man reached for a small box. "Nothing here," he said to the voice. "Probably a bum took a bath. Yeah, I checked real good!"

Soon, the car spun gravel against the curb, and then was out of sight. The city was quiet once more expect for the sound of bubbling water.

"That was close," breathed Lil' Red. "We have to learn to be invisible. There are so many of us. We, as a group, can get loud. Please, watch where you walk."

"Fine," Peppie agreed. "I'm silent."

The others raised a paw then cuddled together to make plans.

Dally spoke, "We need to seek a better place to stay tonight. When morning comes, we can't be in the middle of town."

"Oh you are right!" whimpered Fluffy. "That cop would have found us if he had tried. It nearly scared me to death."

# Chapter 7

"Alright, does anybody know where we are?" asked Lil' Red.

"I do. I used to hang out not far from here. There's a motel with a big fenced yard behind it. It's really a great spot," volunteered Spike. It was starting to rain tiny drops. "If this is going to be a bad day, we should go now and settle in. There's an old building where we can have cover. It's perfect for days."

"Great! Let's go!" Bernie said. "Get on my back Bonnie."

The group stood and waited for others.

"Let me go there first. We need to check it out. I'd hate for us to get there and things be different," demanded Spike.

"Alright, I'm going with you. Mark you come too," yawned Lil' Red. "This way. If things are all right, I'll come back for everybody. If we don't get back, Dally and

Peppie can take lead, and you'll have to find another place."

They departed immediately. Lil' Red worried, "We will need food and water. Bonnie is feeding those babies."

"We'll be alright if it's like it used to be. We just can't be seen. Traveling in a big pack of twenty plus creatures is real difficult. I know where to find food. Water is in a couple buckets there all the time," Spike informed. They had walked over a mile. "See that light? It's over there. Come on!"

He began to run with the two behind him. The opening of the fence was still in place. They rushed through and directly to the shelter in the middle of the big lot. Several old cars were parked there and a big trailer with a lock. They stopped.

"It seems alright," whispered Red. Quickly, three huge screaming cats scattered from the nearby entrance.

"The coast is clear!" rejoiced Spike. "I'll go get the others. Of the cats come back, leave them alone. They won't hurt a thing. They eat mice and frogs. Once they gave me a frog; I was so hungry that day."

Inside the building, there was enough light to reveal a stack of mattresses and other furniture. Lil' Red was excited. "This is worth it! Spike, you're wonderful!"

"Make a place for Bonnie and her babies," smiled Spike with relief. "Mark, come with me; we'll split the group in half. I'll bring some and you bring the others."

They left Lil' Red alone to make a spot for the mother dog. Finishing the little nest in a box, she observed a huge cat coming toward her. It stopped and cocked its back up, hissing and swinging paws.

"Oh cool it!" moaned Red. "We have to stay here tonight. The others will be here soon. We just escaped from the prison of the animal pound. They are going to send all animals there to the medical lab. None of us will bother you. Please understand."

"Oh my!" answered Puss. "I am sorry. I have a litter of kittens up there. Will they be all right? Dogs kill us if we aren't careful."

"No, No, No! Spike already told us about the cats here. He made everyone promise to not bother you. We promise, no cat will be harmed. In fact, if you need something, we'll try to help."

The cat jumped from a barrel of chains and came very close to Red. "How wonderful; I can't go far from my kittens. I want some fish so bad. I really craved them while I was pregnant with the babies."

"We'll get you some fish, one way or another!" promised Red. "This is so good here. How did you find this place?"

"I used to live about a mile from here. I'd explore in the night if the master left me off the screened porch. He didn't like me anyhow. I'd hear him call me 'fat cat', 'fuzz face' and 'puffy *drawers*'. I knew it would be a matter of time that he'd dump me. I met "Cat," a huge white stray. I fell in love at first sight," explained Puss.

"How delightful," smiled Red.

"We moved in together and life was great. Then, I started getting fat and felt bad. He was fine with all of it and we planned a wonderful life." Tears gathered in her eyes. "Cat became real sick himself. He sneezed, wheezed, and laid around real sick. The vet said he had parvovirus. Lots of cats have it. He was almost too late to be helped. I never saw him again. I'm glad I had all my shots. Master did do that for me. It saved me and the babies. Later, we moved here."

The kittens started to cry. Puss looked in their direction. "Are you positive we'll be alright?"

"Absolutely!" agreed Red. "Go feed the little ones. We have a beagle who has puppies. I made this bed for her."

"That is nice. We can be friends. I heard them call you Lil' Red," smiled Puss. "Why are you coming from an animal shelter? You are a beautiful dog."

"I was put there by my madam's son. He was a mean man. He would fuss at *Mumsie* all the time. She was old and slow. I guess she was in his way, you know how people can be," whimpered Red. "Mumsie was so good to me. She'd feed me good things, pet me, and comb me. I felt so happy and loved. They took her off to a nursing home. I didn't get to say good-bye, but I saw the car leave with her and her things."

"How sad. I'll bet she remembers you and misses you too. Love is full of remembering," Puss consoled.

"Yes, I'll always love her," Red said. "That last night before they took her away, old son was yelling worse than ever, saying 'You're old and crippled. I don't have time to come here to fool with you'.

Mumsie cried, "I'm sorry son. I don't mean to be in your way."

Son was drooling at the mouth like he had rabies. 'You ain't going to be in my way no more. I'm taking you to Sunnydale Retirement Center. They can have you! Every time I see you; it's do this, do that. Your stupid dog there, she ain't worth anything. She wouldn't bring a penny at auction! Look at her lay around and eat. Both of you are useless and worthless. Get your junk together. I told them

I'd have you there by seven o'clock. Guess they didn't want to feed you tonight.'

Mumsie whimpered and her eyes turned wet and red. 'Please son, give me another chance. I won't bother you. Lil' Red and I can do just fine.'

'Shut up, old woman! There comes a time for everybody,' he screamed. 'You're old, faded, and ugly.'

'Can I take Red with me?' she wept.

'Of course not… This ain't a party place. You'll have a bed and closet in a room with five other people. Animals ain't allowed. You'll eat in the cafeteria. Lots of people live there and like it. You'll get used to it. If you don't, that's tough stuff!' he growled. 'Get ready. I'll be back soon.'

He drove away and Mumsie put her hands to her face and cried a real long time. She rocked hard in her rocking chair and muttered. 'I never thought son would do me like this. Just leave now. There ain't time for any goodbye.' She cried again."

Lil' Red trembled, "I remember how Mumsie touched me and combed my hair. She gave me baths and good food. I never wanted for anything. I felt safe and had no worries. I was a real pet in every sense of the word."

"My oh my, Red," smiled Puss. "You do have a real story. That life is perfect. At least you had it; some of us are born to misery. I wish all people made us pets like Mumsie did you. We're right tough, but it sure is hell to be punted like a football, then fly through the air ending up in a bush or a wall."

"Yeah, lots of animals are treated cruel and nobody knows," agreed Red. "I say a person that beats and torments an animal could be a wife beater too. Women aren't like men. They are softer by nature and want to nurture us. I suppose it's that nest building thing with them."

"I'd better feed the kittens. I really like you Red," soothed Puss. "You're nice. Oh gosh, here comes a bunch of dogs. Oh, wow, I'll hide out until the coast is clear." The cat jumped over items to return to her high up spot.

# Chapter 8

The room was filled with a bunch of different canines. Spike showed the group in. "Lay down and rest. We need to stay quiet until the others arrive. Lil' Red is the cat still here?"

"Cat? O great, I love to chase cats!" laughed Collie. "They're really a trip – tricky too. Those wiry prongs on the ends of their toes can whack you all over!"

Red walked over and looked at Collie square in the eyes. "You idiot, you're not touching Puss or her babies. Nobody bothers the cat!"

Collie smiled, "Don't kid yourself."

Spike banged his body against Collie. "Red's right! Nobody bothers the cat! Not you, not me, not anybody!"

Collie sat down. "Well, whatever. I suppose she was here first."

"Keep in mind Puss is a good kitty. She has to look after her kittens, and we'll help her." Spike's one ear flipped straight up and the other one dangled giving him a crazy profile. "This is a good place for us to hang out until we think up what we're going to do next. Give Puss and her kittens respect and it will pay off."

Once more, excitement was outside the building. Red stood, "Spike, tell them to cool it. We're not in a barn!"

He rushed outside and gave them directions to be quiet and get inside. Finally, all pound dogs were once more together. The bed prepared for Bonnie and babies was being occupied. The mother dog curled with her back to the wall as her pups were one by one placed by her.

Dally smiled while placing the last pup next to Bonnie's feeding spouts. "The whole family is here now. Look at that sweet little thing. His little pads on his feet look like pink dots."

"Thank you Dal; you're so sweet!" blushed Bonnie.

"Everybody gather around. We need to talk," rushed Red.

"I'm hungry!" whined Chihuahua Peppie. "My belly is yelling!"

"We're all hungry, so listen to Spike. He knows what to do," demanded Lil' Red.

Fluffy cried, "I'm so scared. Suppose somebody finds us, we are in a worse mess than ever!"

Spike stood. "We are on a mission of life. We have escaped a death that would for sure come within a few weeks. We can't backtrack, or even think of anything except today. Tomorrow will come soon enough."

"Mr. Spike, you know the area. We need food," growled Bernie the Saint Bernard.

Mix Breed chuckled, "I'm sure it'll take a horse to feed you enough."

Spike cut in, "It's still dark. We need to gather food now. I know where to go and bring it back here. Four of us will search – Babe, Mark, Dally, and me."

The group quickly left. Once they were outside, it was apparent speed was vital. "The hotel restaurant has good stuff sometimes; it will be straight ahead. They have a guard, but he stays out front with some pretty woman at a tall table," informed Spike.

In minutes, they were beside the restaurant dumpster. Mark grumbled, "There isn't a thing in here!"

"Sh-sh-sh! Hold on. See that big hole? Let me stand on your back and look," whispered Spike.

"All right, but we're wasting time!" griped Mark.

"Try it, dumb-bell" demanded Babe. "I smell meat!"

Once in place, on top of Mark, Spike smiled widely. "It'll be a hot time in the old town tonight! They have had a party. Holy mercy It's a feast! My mouth is watering! I'm going in. I'll throw what I can outside, then we'll take it back."

He forced himself inside the huge metal box. A huge container of bread broke his fall, but not his spirit. HE began grabbing all the prime rib bones he could find, slinging them outside. The others marveled as they saw the wonderful meaty bones fly to them.

"Oh Spike, this is fabulous!" yelled Babe, licking one.

"Sh-sh-sh! Start taking all you can back to the others and hurry back," cautioned Mark. "We need to store up all we can tonight. Don't eat now; we have to hurry."

The others obeyed and dropped their prizes at the feet of the waiting group. Babe smiled, "We have to get back for more. Don't hog it all up!"

"We won't eat anything until everybody is here," promised Lil' Red. "Except Bonnie beagle. She's feeding six!"

The runners returned to the dumpster and grabbed all they could handle. This was repeated many times more.

On the last trip to their refuge they were showing their exhaustion.

"We'd better have some other dogs make this nexttrip," suggested Fluffy. "You guys are going to croak."

"I ain't a frog, but I could use a rest. My legs hurt. I'm not so young anymore!" Babe laughed.

"I'm going!" insisted Bernie. "I can carry more than any of you. Let's go. I see the dumpster over there."

He bound out like a miniature bear. Two mix breeds followed, with Peppie running along. She was so fast she arrived at the container ahead of the others. "Hey Spike, we're back. Those other dogs had to rest. Here comes big Bernie!"

"Great! I threw that box out and filled it up. Maybe he can haul it. There's lots of bags of bread. It's not great, but it will stop a stomach growl."

"Bread is alright. People always put stuff between pieces and call them sandwiches," grinned Peppie. "I smell fish. Is there fish in there?"

"Yeah, a pile of it," he laughed. "I set it aside for Puss."

"The cat? That silly pussy cat that has us all in jitters?" squeaked Peppie.

"She's my friend. I've known her for years. Trust me you'll learn to love her."

"Humph! Love is a strong word for thoughts of a cat. I swore off the things after one connected with my nose. Their claws are like razors! I've taken that pill just one time too many!" grunted Bernie trying to hoist the big full box. "Put it like this; play like cats are eggs. Just leave them alone and nothing breaks."

"You're huge. You could take any cat down." Peppie jumped in front of Bernie.

"Just because I'm big, it doesn't make me a murderer. You are about the size of Puss. I wouldn't hurt you. You live and let live. Right now I need you to help me get this box going. What can we do?"

"We need a handle on it, Bernie. Look over there, that long stick."

"A broom handle?" Bernie questioned.

"Sure. A bucket does this. We'll make this box like a bucket. "I'll chew a hole in each side and we'll put the stick through."

Quickly, Peppie clawed enough to start a hole on one side. She finished off making a hole on each side.

"Well, I do declare! You are sharp!" exclaimed Bernie pushing the stick through the holes. You're a genie!"

"No, it's the Mexican in me!" laughed the small dog.

# Chapter 9

From inside the dumpster Mark watched Bernie leave. "Hurry back big boy; we can chance only one more trip! The people get out of work and new ones will come. Just hurry!"

With everyone moving the food the task was soon complete and the refuge of the shed was now a new home.

"Oh my gosh!" whined Fluffy. "We've been dumb. As people say, 'you can't live by bread alone'; we don't have water. That jug of milk will have to be saved for Puss and Bonnie. I'm thirsty now!"

Puss walked out overhead and lay on a rafter. "Never fear, Puss is here!"

All the dogs laughed together.

Puss pointed, "Look there!"

All heads turned to a large old tub. It was empty. Their hearts fell with disappointment.

"Yes, but there's no water!" cried Zipper.

"But the water is not far away. Move that tub outside the entrance first, and I'll tell you about water," giggled Puss.

"That's right!" Mark praised. That snake looking thing out there near the bush will give water sometimes.

"What does it do? Vomit?" asked Fluffy.

"No, Nut, there's a knob somewhere. A man that works out there turns it. He likes me so I'll get him to turn it on. That 'snake' has two bodies. We'll put one in our tub and let the other one stay where it is," Puss planned. She could see daylight beginning. "We'd better hurry. Cover that snake after you move it. We don't want anybody to notice."

"I know where to look. My hair color blends with the turf. I'll do this," Spike insisted.

"Go to that big Camellia bush. Be careful," ordered Puss. "Pull the longest end to here and put it in the water catcher. I hope it will reach."

Spike shot to where the hose was rolled in a pile. He could barely see it from the fallen debris. It had an odd head on it; round metal with a push button on the end. Taking the end and pulling hard was easy at first. He smiled to himself and decided to run with the end while the others watched.

It was hard for everyone to see out the door. Suddenly, Puss screamed, "Slow down, Nut, you're …"

The warning was too late. Spike came to the end of the hose at full speed. It was like a whip. The giant snake slung him head over heel onto the ground on his back. It knocked the breath out of him. He felt like a fool with his eyes rolling around in his head and tongue hanging bleeding. He never wanted to face the others. He thought he'd play dead and slink away when nobody watched.

"My gracious! Spike has killed himself!" cried Fluffy. "Look, he isn't moving!"

"The fool was showing off," giggled Puss. "If he's not alive we'll just eat him for breakfast!"

Spike heard the "eat" and came to his feet. He thought, 'The good thing about being a dog is nobody can see you red-faced from embarrassment. Thank God for face hair.'

Puss ordered, "You've got the 'snake' hooked on a stump. Untangle it and hurry."

Peppie rushed to his rescue, "Let me help."

They pulled the long snake into place adjusting the tub so it would fit.

"Purr-fect!" smiled Puss. "We'll have water soon. If it rains, there will be lots of water."

"I'd love a bath," whispered Fluffy. "I just love being all soapy and sweet smelling."

"Yeah it would be nice," agreed Bonnie. "My babies need to learn to keep clean."

"That will all come later," Puss purred. "Somebody has to make the snake pour water. It's over there against that big rock."

"Let me take a look," Peppie volunteered and slipped to the spot in a flash. "I found it, but I can't budge it. It's real tight."

"You don't weigh but eight pounds. It will take somebody big!" Fluffy said. I wish I were strong."

"I'll try!" Dally stood. "At the fire station we have to work with big water lines. I used to help before they passed the law to get rid of the truck-dog."

Dally solved the problem quickly. Standing back it was easy to see the flow from the snake's mouth. "You did it, Dal! Now things will be good," Puss praised.

Dal noticed a cup near the building. He grabbed it between his teeth and dipped it in the water that was filling the big container. Carefully, he took it inside and smiled. "Look! Real water. It's beautiful. Puss, you need the first drink."

"Thank you. I really need water for me and the kittens," she said.

"Come get your reward. None of us will ever hurt you ... " began Dal.

"Nor chase? Nor fool with my kittens?" added Puss. "Let me see a show of tails!"

Pledging to befriend the cat, all the dogs stood and flipped their tails straight in the air. There were short ones, long ones, skinny ones and real furry ones. They all agreed. Puss was special and a friend.

# Chapter 10

The animals had managed to pull together and set up a home. Spike and Puss were proven. They earned respect from their peers by sharing their domain.

"Everyone has to be somewhere," Peppie smiled as she rolled onto her back stretching in a warm sunbeam piercing through a crack in the wall. "My oh my, this feels good. This sure is a great place to be."

They agreed the food was good. Even Puss was still licking her front paws with satisfaction. "Milk and fish! What a treat!" she purred profoundly.

"You should have the best. You held the fort down for a long time. That was dumb of me to go away with that boy. His parents had a flying hissy fit. They put me on a chain and called the animal squad," Spike informed.

"So that's what happened," mused Puss.

"It took a few days before the cops came. When they arrived, I was gone with the boys in blue." He stared at the door. Suddenly he jumped. "What's that?"

Moving quietly, they tried to get a look in the direction from a loud blast from outside. Mark, Babe, and Spike gazed with ears erect and hearts pounding. Babe broke the silence. "Well, pinch my greyhound tail! Look out there! The world is coming to an end!"

"Look at the fire!" cried Fluffy peeking under the long-legged animals. "What do we do?"

"Be cool," required Lil' Red. "We must stay calm and make a plan."

Spike spoke, "It's over there but it could change. This building has a place underneath. We'd better go there."

"Exactly!" Dal registered. "When I went to the elementary schools with Captain, they taught kids to get out and stay low. They made me 'stop, drop and roll' to show the children what to do if caught on fire."

"We aren't on fire but we need to be out of here if they come to look around," Lil' Red decided. "We have to move all babies first. Puss, the smaller dogs can carry some kittens for you!"

"Pur-r-r-r-fic! Ya-y-y'll be gentle!" she continued. "Their toes are like mini razors. I'll drop them on that straw there. Grab them and run!"

"We have to hide quickly while we can," Red ordered. "Babies first, small dogs then you big pooches!"

"I hope I can get flat to the ground. I'm huge!" complained Bernie the Saint Bernard.

"You'll be alright," Spike acknowledged. "We'll just make ourselves invisible."

"I'm scared of mice and rats!" whimpered Fluffy.

"Don't sweat that! I'm in charge of mice extermination," laughed Puss. "Here, take this kitten."

As the kitten dropped in front of Fluffy in the straw she gleed, "Gee, what a cute little thing, I've never seen such a cute ball of cotton."

"Hurry, Nut, take it by the loose skin on its neck and get it down under," pushed Red. The group soon cleared the upper level and lay on the dirty ground beneath their home. They were each feeling the burning flames of the dumpster. The flames became bigger and again there was a real big explosion that wiggled the dumpster. Flames blew high and pieces flew through the air setting leaves and papers on fire. This created a greater fire area.

Dal jumped, "I've gotta get help. Everybody stay here!"

He raced to the main door at the lobby of the hotel. An electric eye opened the door. Without thought he rushed to the clerk and stood with his front paws on the desk as if renting a room.

The woman turned quickly and shrieked, "What do You want? You beast! Get outta here!"

The dog was trying to force her to understand. He jumped all the way onto the desk then over. He sat dropped to the ground and rolled. As he repeated the "Stop, drop and roll' a family of four came from the back elevator. Hearing them, Dal raced to the two children. He quickly did his "Stop, drop and roll."

"Look, he's the fire department dog!" cried a little boy.

"Be careful, he might bite!" warned the clerk.

"No, he will not! He's telling us something!" screamed the child. "What is it boy?"

Dal moved to the child taking his hand in his mouth. He wished he could say it in human words but whined, "Come with me!"

He added a little pressure and motioned with his head toward the door. The family followed. Once around the side of the building they could see the beginning of a massive fire.

The child screamed, "See! He told us! He's a perfect dog daddy!"

The father reached to his hip and dialed "911" with the information given on the phone, it was only minutes before the fire sirens were coming from all directions. This made Dal's blood surge with excitement. He sat a moment then pulled the boy away and rushed inside the hotel with him. The rest of the family followed.

Once more, the father relayed the fire situation to the desk clerk.

"That dog has saved our hotel!" she screamed as she pushed all the alarms to alert everyone in the hotel. "What a dog!"

Immediately, the firefighters were on the scene. Trucks were blaring their horns and whistles and staged their flashing red lights as if vibrant dancing flames.

Firefighters rushed onto the scene with tremendous 'snakes' that ultimately placed a storm of violent streams over the flames in the dumpster and the side of the hotel. Their precision changed the flames into heavy plumes of smoke that darkened the sky. Soon it diminished to zero flames and smelly smoke.

Hotel personnel and guest had been directed to the swimming pool area. They were joined by onlookers and finally a television crew. Several hours later the emergency was at rest.

A cameraman was panning his lens around the crowd. The close-up shot revealed a small boy with a well-spotted Dalmatian. A woman with a stick in her hand rushed over and a small red light appeared. She smiled widely and flipped her hair. Dal's nose wiggled as he caught a whiff of her sweet perfume.

"Son, I understand you and your dog discovered the fire," she stated as if asking a question.

"He found it ma-am. He's a smart dog," replied the child.

"Oh! What is your name and your dog's name?"

"My, uh, uh, name is Isaac, but this isn't my dog. He just ran into the lobby," he answered. "He made us follow him."

"A dog? This dog, oh my! He is truly a hero!" she exclaimed.

"Lady, he is a Dalmatian. They are taught to know about firefighting," he told her.

"Where did he come from?" the reporter inquired.

"I reckon he was walking his beat just like policemen do," answered Isaac.

"Amazing!" laughed the pretty reporter. "Amazing! Is this dog a part of the fire unit out here?" She directed the questions to a firefighter who was securing the area.

The man stopped and smiled. Snapping his fingers, he motioned to Dal. "He used to be with the fire department. We had to send him away from service. The city council voted 'No dogs' but you can certainly see his value. Had this dog not been trained to act, this hotel would have been gone. Fire travels fast. This fire was only minutes from being very serious."

Did he really save this hotel?" she gasped.

"Yes, he certainly did and most likely lives too. Let me say 'Thank you' Dal. I hope you'll come back to us at the station."

Dal smiled showing his teeth. He shook his head up and down then ran from the set. Once outside, he raced to return to the others under the shed. He was panting with excitement.

"Dal, you were great!" bragged Lil' Red. "We're proud of you. If the fire department will hire you back, we want you to go. After all, that's where your heart is."

"Thanks, that won't happen. I did love the department and the crew. Right now, I'm happy to be here!" Dally insisted. He settled with a faraway look in his eyes.

He kept watching the final cleanup until the last truck swept its way from the front of the hotel. Dal felt tears fill his eyes. His buddies would be gone and once more he'd be on his own.

# Chapter 11

The next morning the sun seemed to rise extra early. "I'm going to run out for a few minutes before the town gets busy," whispered Peppie.

"Good! I'll come along!" replied Lil' Red.

As they eased out their little entrance, Spike grunted, "Wait, you might get lost. I'm coming!"

The three slipped through a crack in the fence out back. There was no traffic but birds were chirping loudly. Red looked up at a power pole. "Watch it! That's nasty!"

The other two grinned as she rolled in the grass to remove the bird poo. Quickly she joined Spike and Peppie. "Spike, you know this town. What do you think we can do? We can't stay forever in the shed. Everything changes. It's an end or a beginning."

"That's true," sniffed Peppie. "I'm not a bad dog. I just got lost and can't find my way home. I had been adopted two times from the pound but nobody loved me much.

One man had to move to Seattle and I couldn't go. He left me with his neighbor. They got rid of me to the Sunnydale Animal Shelter. I was there three weeks until somebody else took me. It seemed to go real well. They had a little girl. I would play with her, but she teased me a lot. That made me grouchy. The little girl's father was afraid my teeth might somehow hook onto the child."

"That's the way people are. We're like some kind of toy to some humans. They hug and kiss on us one minute then, you're flying through the air like a punted football!" Spike panted.

"The kid's mother found me a wonderful home. I went to a woman that owns a clothing store. That's a great place. She spoiled me silly. She gave me everything a dog could need. I had all kinds of toys, and I mean great stuff, huge box full. She would grill T-bones for me. I'm telling you, it was dog heaven! The best home any dog could dream for. I even had a full wardrobe of clothes, towels, rugs, every cage under the sun," Peppie boasted. "I even slept with her in a nice soft king-size bed with feathers and satin covered pillows."

"Wow! How on earth did you get lost?" Spike asked.

Peppie burped, "I was outside in the park. A woman ran me down, and caught me and took me off in her car. I could see Miss Rosie as we drove off, but she looked in another direction for me. Anyhow, when I got to the grocery store with the woman, I ran away. A cop picked me up. The rest is history."

"You should have stayed back at the kennel, Peppie," decided Lil' Red. "That woman is probably still looking for you. She loved you and I'm certain she wanted you. "

"I don't know. I had been at the rescue a week I believe," squinted Peppie.

"Sometimes it takes more time to connect," smiled Spike.

"Really! Do you think so? They were going to get rid of all of us, don't you remember? I was scared to stay," Peppie reminded them.

"Somehow, we'll find Miss Rosie. We'll start looking every night," Spike promised.

"Hey! Look at this!" screamed Lil' Red.

"Oh, gracious!" exclaimed Spike.

"Wow!" squealed Peppie.

They stood before a newspaper rack and stared at the most beautiful picture of a Dalmatian.

"It's him! That's our Dal!" Peppie cried.

"Yes! It's Dal! Look at that big red truck!" giggled Lil' Red. "He's beside it. That truck was at our fire. We'll get a copy and take it home!"

"Dunce, you can't get that picture out of that thing!" snarled Peppie. "Those machines are metal."

"I know how to find one! Follow me!" ordered Spike.

The three scampered a few blocks down the street. Several unopened stores had a roll of papers by their door. "See that?" smiled Spike. "We'll have to get one of them. People get newspapers at their door."

"Are you sure? We just take one?" questioned Peppie.

"I hate to take something from somebody that's not thrown away. I can bring it back later," promised Spike. He looked at a trashcan beside a little coffee shop. "Wait! Look here! We're in luck."

On the can was the cover picture of Dal. "This was meant to be! I expect somebody trashed it after their morning coffee," delighted Lil' Red.

"I'll grab it quickly and we'll go back," Spike volunteered. "I'm tallest."

"Oh, mercy! Smell those donuts!" Peppie licked her lips. The aroma drifted through the air. "I love cinnamon, chocolate and nuts. Sniff it! Isn't that wonderful?"

"Oh yes!" agreed Lil' Red.

"We can't have everything!" Spike nodded; then reached into the can for the newspaper. As he pulled from the wire container, he spotted a nice box. Quickly, he threw the paper to Lil' Red and grabbed the box with his huge wide-open wolf-like mouth. When his feet touched the sidewalk, he rushed to a nearby path between buildings. The others trotted behind him. He placed it on the ground and forced the top off.

"Oh Spike! Donuts – Krispy Kreme too! Please can I have one?" drooled Peppie.

"Eat all you want. There's more boxes; I'll get them!" He smiled, feeling a thrill from making Peppie's wish come true. "We'll take some to the others."

"We'll go with you. I can't eat without you," Peppie said.

"No, let me bring what I can. We can't all be seen getting into the trash. Trust me," he ordered.

It didn't take long until he had brought about ten boxes full of donuts into the alleyway.

"I found this piece of cloth. We can stretch it out. Put all the boxes on it then roll them up and carry it like a stretcher," Lil' Red advised.

"Brilliant!" Spike gleed.

Soon they were on their way back to the building behind the hotel. "Wait! The picture of Dal!" screamed Spike.

"Don't worry! We have it right here!" grinned Red. The picture was on top the boxes.

Soon they were inside the fence and back into the safety of their newfound home. Their excitement awakened those who were not awake. Puss was feeding her half-wild kittens and Bonnie was playing with her puppies.

"Quiet, can't a body sleep anymore?" yawned the giant of a dog.

"You'll love this!" squealed Peppie flipping her tiny Chihuahua body onto his huge paws. "We have a special breakfast, Bernie! Look, donuts! Better still, look at this picture of Dal!"

They stood around the newspaper gazing at the beautiful spotted dog picture on the front page with one word at the top - "HERO."

# Chapter 12

It rained constantly for several days. This made finding food more difficult. The shed was still a good temporary home.

Puss called out to her kittens, "Me-ooow! Come here!"

They quickly gathered around rubbing against each other and their mother. She announced, "I'm bringing the babies down. They need more room to romp. I need to feed them something besides my milk, too!"

"Bring 'em on!" snickered Spike. "This should be fun!"

"Oh yeah?" hissed the mother cat. "Do you see these razor sharp claws on the end of my ten fingers? Bother my children and you'll find out the meaning of 'spike'!"

"N-no, I-I promise, I'll look after them. D-don't you remember, I-I brought you th-that fish," stuttered Spike. He hated for anyone to see him tremble yet the idea of connecting with cat claws put the fear of God in him.

Puss felt satisfaction, watching him quiver. If he were a human, sweat would be pouring off his face. She connected directly into his eyes as she moved in front of him. Spike continued to shake; he slid to the floor feeling foolish.

"You and this whole pack of rats had better look after these babies. They are tiny and ready to learn. I expect each of you to cat-sit and help me," scoffed Puss. She stuck one of her long lanky back legs high in the air and gently brushed it with her tongue.

Bonnie walked to her face and smiled. "Pussy Cat, I'm in the same boat with you. Look over there!"

Everyone's eyes followed the pointed finger. The five puppies were flopped together in a pile on the floor asleep.

"So what, idiot! Look up there!" Puss pointed. All eyes again watched in amazement. Five fluffy kittens leaned against each other on a rafter. "How do you expect those fat little hound dogs to accept my children?'

Bonnie smiled, we set an example. We are mothers and we can teach the babies."

"Teach? How do you teach what is nature? Cat is cat; kitten is kitten; dog is dog; pup is pup!" screamed Puss. "We are what we are, dumb ox!"

"That's true. Come here," motioned Bonnie.

Puss stood on all fours in front of the beagle, face-to-face, eye-to-eye.

"It starts here, me and you, us," Bonnie whimpered. "We can fight and be miserable or we can be friends. There is so much to gain with being friends. Different is no excuse. I'll bet if we let our babies get together now before they learn that 'difference,' they can be friends too."

"It's a bet!" snapped Puss. "If they can get along without us making them accept each other, I'll get you a steak.

"Fine, I'll get you fish if they don't!" challenged Bonnie.

Puss raced to the skywalk above. She smiled, "Meow, come kittens; I want you to meet the puppies!" Bonnie crawled to her pup babies, "Wake up, the kittens are coming. Just watch over there. They can be nice playmates."

The five tiny puppies squirmed and stretched. Sitting up, they yawned and stuck their feet in the air. Bonnie proudly washed each one's sweet cute face. They waited.

It was as if a magic wand had swept over the whole place. All the varied dogs were silent and sitting anxiously waiting for the next move Puss would make.

Movement overhead with heavy dust falling was the first phase of the feline's descent. In the distance church bells were playing a melody. Puss motioned for her babies to follow to the music as if on stage at a pageant. They had all walked the narrow overhead board. Soon the kittens were jumping and rolling along the footsteps of their mother. Occasionally, a kitten would meow.

"Wow! Aren't they beautiful!" puffed the poodle Fluffy. "So little, so cute, so striped!" I just want to pet one! I believe I could really love a cat!"

"Hush!" whispered Beagle. "Come on Puss, my pups are waiting!"

"Go on!" demanded Puss pushing her first kitten.

Quickly the baby hunched its back and hissed. The fine hair on his back stood straight up.

The five puppies stared in fear and began to tremble. It was as if a monster had appeared. When the kitten looked back, he could see his mother's smile of 'okay.' Relaxing, he watched the puppies. They cuddled together and trembled.

"All right, Bonnie," muttered Puss. "It's time for us to act like we are friends."

"Of course. What do we do? Shall I kiss you, girlfriend?" snickered the beagle.

"I don't know if we need to go that far. Maybe I'll come to you and sniff your ears like you dogs do," Puss suggested.

"That should work!" gleed Beagle stretching her head forward. "Do it!"

"Well, I hope you smell good. I've never been this close to a canine." The mother cat cocked her head and sat immediately in front of Bonnie the dog. Quickly, she stuck her head out and sniffed the dog. "Wow! How interesting; you're not bad at all. You want to sniff my ears?"

"Sure!" smiled the beagle, as she leaned forward to connect her nose to the cat's face. Their whiskers twitched as they touched. "You're so soft, Puss."

The mother dog and mother cat kept touching each other's face to discover their *differences*. The cat purred with pleasure and the mother dog gently whined. Puss kept rubbing against the black, tan and white Beagle with excitement.

"You aren't as different as I thought," cat surmised. "Friends?"

Bonnie took her hand and connected with the outreached paw of Puss. The dog smiled, "Oh, yes! Friends!"

Quickly, the kittens rushed to Puss. They rubbed all over their mother all *mee-owing* at once. They would fall over laughing showing off for the puppies who were looking on.

The baby dogs reluctantly gathered around their mother. Bonnie lapped each one lovingly with her tongue. The babies kept watching the kittens in amazement. Bonnie coaxed. "See the new friends. You can play with them."

Puss spoke to her kittens, "Go ahead, play with the puppies."

The largest kitten smiled, "Me-ooow!" Quickly she eased to the group of puppies and said, "Friends? Me-oow!"

She playfully rubbed one of the pups. The puppy rolled over on his back and the kitten began to lick his belly. The little dog's eyes crossed with pleasure.

All the ten baby animals joined together in an easy wrestling and rolling game. They rushed around in play chasing tails and jumping on each other.

Bonnie and Puss smiled contently together, "We both won!"

"I'll get you a steak!" gleed Puss.

"I'll find you some fish!" answered Bonnie. "This will make life easier for us. It really shows, you learn to love as a baby. I respect you and that is good."

Lil' Red started singing, "For they are jolly good fellows."

The rest of the dogs joined in. Their happy song ended in a multi-pitched, "Nobody can't deny!"

Outside the building, someone was emptying kitchen trash. The old man smiled to himself hearing the happy notes. He separated the chicken, fish and steak by laying it onto a long cardboard box. With a big whistle, he called, "Hey out there. Come and get it!"

He went back to the kitchen. The animals followed his whistle and invitation. They bolted out their doorway.

Spike marveled, "Wow! Look at that!"

"Did this come from heaven?" Bernard gruffly asked.

"No, the kitchen man is good like this," Spike informed. "Tonight, he's good, but tomorrow he may change. We'll eat well tonight, but we'd better plan to leave here soon. Too many people know 'dogs' are here; we'll soon get caught!"

"You're probably right," Lil' Red agreed. "We had better take this food inside."

# Chapter 13

Light from a big full moon lit the grounds within the fence behind the motel. The outside lights were barely visible. It was already 2:00 A.M.

"I can't sleep!" wiggled Fluffy. "I like it better dark. That big light bulb out there will never shut off."

"Silly, that's the moon. It's a full moon not a light," informed Peppie.

"Oh! What do we do? I'm scared of this kind of light," whined the white poodle. I can't sleep under cover like you."

"Gracious girl. All you do is cover your head. I roll up in blankets and keep my whole self-covered," said Zipper. "I used to have a special quilt that was all mine when I was at David and Becky's house. I loved them so much. They rescued me from a dog pound in another county."

"Really?" asked Lil' Red. "Me and you are both Dachshunds. You're black and a miniature and I'm a standard. I agree, I love rolling into a ball of fabric."

"I used to visit that dress shop in town," laughed Zipper. "Becky's mother owned it and I stayed with her for a week. This one day, I got into the showroom window and found a beautiful beaded white long-tailed dress on a false person. Well that 'dummy' didn't need the 'tail' so I rolled up into it and basked for several hours in the sun... right there in the big fancy window."

"You didn't!" giggled Lil' Red.

"I did until some old tall girl came roaring in the door screaming, 'Miss Rose! Miss Rose! Come here quick! Yo' has a rat in yo' window!' I laid real still," relayed Zipper.

"Oh gosh, what happened? Were you in trouble?" sniffed Lil' Red.

"Not really. About a dozen people came flying to look. Unfortunately, my nose was sticking out. Miss Rose just laughed and said, 'That's my grand dog! Everyone thought it was cool. I just got deeper into the tail and went back to sleep."

"How nice. Some people are so understanding," Lil' Red sighed. "That's a wonderful story."

"Zipper!" Peppie addressed. "You said, a dress shop. The woman was Miss Rose. Is that Rosie?"

"Yeah, Rose, Rosie ... they used to call her both," answered Zipper.

"What a little world. I used to live there! A dress shop! Yes, Rosie's Dress Shop! We are kin-dogs by people. She was my master, my human mommie! Oh Zipper! I love you! Did she feed you Pedigree in the purple pouch?" cried Peppie.

"Yes! Oh yes, isn't that wonderful stuff! The clothes, did you ever get clothes?" asked Zipper. "I had a black and white striped sweater."

"I did too! We are kin-dogs!" cried Peppie with tears rolling down her cheeks. "Rosie said she had a wonderful grand dog and we were going to see each other soon!"

The two were so delighted with their find. They sniffed each other and raced around the shack so happily.

"Calm down you fools!" snapped Lil' Red. People are going to hear you."

"We can't help it. It's so wonderful to find each other," grinned Peppie. "I wish we could find Rosie. I'm sure she's here somewhere. I'll bet she looked for me after I got snatched away from her."

"You're right," Zipper agreed. "You are very right. If we find Rosie, she can find Becky and David. If we go out looking, we could find her place."

"It would be so great if you could go home. It's so awful to be homeless," cried Lil' Red. "We want you to go look. Do you remember the town fountain where we were when we first left the *dog pound*?"

"I don't know how to get there," quivered Zipper.

"Spike, you know the town; take them on a stroll," Lil' Red ordered. "Do you know where they sell those people clothes?"

"I can try. I don't pay attention to anything I can't eat," he laughed.

"Golly, Spike ... will you help us?" squealed Peppie. "I really want my momma!" Tears swelled into her eyes.

"Of course, you're so cute, anyone would about die if you got gone from them. We can look for Rosie's place now!" offered Spike.

"Oh, Spike! Thank you, thank you! I'll love you forever!" Peppie grinned and rolled over and over.

"Spike, just take one of them. You can't take the chance of too many 'strays' being seen at one time," suggested Lil' Red.

"Peppie, you stay here. Zipper can help me. We'll come back for you. I promise," Spike licked her nose and rubbed her belly with his head.

"All right, just please find my Rosie!" she sniffed.

Zipper and Spike departed. They went straight to the water fountain area. It was cool with a slight breeze.

"I'm kinda cold," Zipper whispered. "I'm eleven years old; that makes me older than you. I don't have much hair anymore. Look at my tail it's almost a stick."

Spike laughed, "I like your little tail. Dig my ear that flops; it's me though! My flopping ear is my trademark!"

"You are so smart to know where everything is. Being on the streets has sure made you street-smart," gloried Zipper, as they trudged on.

"Yeah, but street-smart and alone is a cold lonely life sometimes. People don't really like mix-breeds. I can't help being all mixed up. My momma was chained in a yard and a mix-breed visited her. I really don't know my father," Spike sadly told him. "I'm always homeless."

"Spike, if you can find Rosie I'll try to get David and Becky to let you come live with us. I was their only child. I can always get my way with Becky. She's a pushover when I shower her with attention," invited Zipper.

"Wow! That would be fantastic! I've never really had a home or that love stuff you're talking about," replied the large unique mostly white dog. "Come on, let's cross the street."

"At least I know how to stay out of roads. I listen carefully, but my eyesight isn't great. Sh! Sh! Sh!" whispered Zipper. He ran behind Spike and jumped into a bush with him. "Listen!"

"I don't hear anything!" Spike exclaimed. "What is it?"

"Hush! Footsteps!" Zipper warned as they watched.

Very soon a policeman stopped almost in front of them. He slipped a piece of gum in his mouth then moved on. A funny sound came from his hip. They watched him snap a box from his belt and talk.

"Everything's fine out here. I shook all the doors. You've got to see that new dress in the window at Rosie's shop. It's fantastic! I've never seen anything sparkle so. My girlfriend will look tough in that!" he bragged. "Yeah, pick me up."

He stood by the curb waiting. Soon, a marked car stopped. He grunted as he wrestled inside.

Zipper leaned against Spike, "You heard that!"

"Rosie's Dress Shop should be that way," decided Spike, pointing. "The policeman came from there."

"Right! Let's go!" Zipper squeaked.

"We have to be sure the coast is clear," panted Spike. "We're too close now."

They peeked all around. The big moon made it easy. Nothing was moving.

"We need to go down that alley. Would you know her place from the back side?" Spike pondered.

"Maybe, I used to go out back to 'potty' and the trash cans out there always have bunches of flowers in them." Zipper grinned. "What a dream come true. Peppie will go nuts!"

"I can see her now. She runs all over like a maniac ... wild and in circles. She's so cute when she gets happy," the other dog chuckled. "Come on!"

The two scampered down the alley. A huge white cat jumped in front of them. He arched his back, hissed, then grow led deep from his throat.

Spike laughed, "Hey, buddy, we have to hurry…"

"Hurry? Who do you think you are? This is my block," snarled the huge cat. "Get outta here, now!"

Zipper shivered, "Sir, I used to visit near here. We're just trying to find Rosie. The dress shop where my little kin-dog lived. We all got lost. Poor little Peppie was 'snatched' from Rosie's place. She ended up at the pound with all of us."

"The pound? Are you some of those dogs the city is looking for? Did you dig out one night?" quizzed Cat arching his eyebrows.

"We had to do it. They were going to send us off to a med-lab," injected Spike. "They were not waiting for anyone to come except us. We were soon to be a void piece of history."

"The whole town is talking about you. How fantastic that you slipped the shaft to them before they did it to you! I love it!" giggled White Cat. "Come on, I'll take you to Rosie's store. Would you believe she puts tuna out for me sometimes? I like her so much that I never sit on top of her car."

"A white cat being so kind must be a sign of *good luck*; like a black cat is bad luck if it walks in front of you," surmised Zipper. "Can you really take us there, to Rosie?"

"I'll try, but I need a favor back," Cat grinned.

"Oh yes, anything!" pleaded Zipper.

"We'll sure try!" Spike agreed.

"I lost my girlfriend, a beautiful Calico. She ran away some time ago. I haven't seen her since. I'll bet she is still around somewhere," the handsome white feline sighed.

"If you'll help me, that's all I can expect. Two eyes aren't as good as six."

It didn't take long before Zipper began to run and whine. "Oh my goodness! Oh my goodness! It's Rosie's shop. Isn't it beautiful! It's heaven. I'm found! I'm found! I'm found! Peppie is found! Oh mercy! Peppie is found!"

"Not so fast, buddy!" worried Spike. "Now we have to find our way to the shack."

"We will, we will!" bubbled Zipper throwing his leg ' up' against a bush. "We just have to find the fountain. We go back that way, cross the road and go back to the fountain then to the shack."

"Oh, I guess so but it's getting too light. We can't be seen," reminded Spike.

"I know where the fountain is. There's that music clock there, isn't it?" White Cat quizzed.

"That's it! That's it!" jumped Zipper with glee.

"Come on, I'll show you. Now you really owe me!" pointed out Cat. "It's this way!"

The three marched in a line in a different direction.

"You sure this is the way?" asked Zipper.

# Chapter 14

It was becoming daylight. The clock bonged six times and played a song, "Oh What a Beautiful Morning!" The three creatures rushed into some high bushes beside the fountain.

"We made it! Oh thank you Mr. Cat. You are brilliant," Spike praised. "Please come on to our shack. We have lots of food and water. The rest of our dog friends are there."

"How many?"

"Maybe twenty!"

"Oh, that might not be so good!" reneged the cat.

"Oh come on, it will be fine. The others will take you in. You've been a lifesaver already," pleaded Spike. "I'll give you my word - nobody will touch you!"

Reluctantly, Cat agreed to continue the return with his newfound buddies. Once more, Spike urged the others to follow. "It won't be a long walk. We'll be there in minutes. We have to tell Peppie the good news. She will flip!"

Swiftly, the three safely made their way to the shack. A rooster on a nearby fence stretched and screamed over and over, "Cock-a-doodle-doo! The sun is looking for you!" In the distance, a huge cow shook her body and called back, "Moo-uh-uh-uh-ooow! I'm awake too!"

Sir Cat twitched his whiskers, "I'll wait outside. I always like to be announced. It's fitting for strangers."

Spike assured, "I understand. Hang on!"

Zipper rushed inside beaming, "Peppie! Oh Peppie! We found Rosie! We did! We did! We found Rosie's store!"

The little Chihuahua jumped to her feet, "I knew it! We're found! We're found! Oh, Zipper! Zipper!"

With this, the two went nearly nuts. They rolled and jumped, hugged and kissed and raced around, both exclaiming over and over their happiness.

"This is good!" exclaimed Lil' Red. "It's time for us to look to the future for each of us. It has been good being together, but sooner or later, we will be discovered. God forbid!"

Spike rubbed Lil' Red gently with his head. "Pretty lady in red, you are so strong. You've held us all together. This is the beginning; we'll all find homes."

Lil' Red felt sad, "Mumsie is gone. I'll never go home."

"Look, we'll take it a day at a time. Don't grieve; just have faith. Peppie and Zipper are found. In fact, we met a wonderful creature who helped us find Rosie's store. Brace yourselves friends and Lil' Red – meet Sir Cat, the Magnificent! Ta-dah!"

Zipper yelled, "Drum roll! Dah-ah!"

With a glorious smile and flashing pearly white teeth that sparkled like jewels embedded in a cloud of white, Sir Cat stepped inside.

You could hear the gasping while the group stared.

"My goodness!" whispered Fluffy. "It's a *cat* in my coat!"

"Cat?" squealed the group. Suddenly, every dog's hair stood on end.

"Yes, it's a cat, you idiots," Lil' Red growled. A big fine cat that helped Zipper and Spike, that makes him family! This white cat is now family!"

Puss sacheted beside Lil' Red and put her hands on her hips. She smiled, flipping her lashes, "Hello big boy!"

Sir Cat dropped to the floor, "Miss Puss, it's you! I can't believe this; my beautiful kitty. I've missed you so much! Why did you leave me?"

Puss rubbed her whole body against him and snapped her tail from side to side. Quickly, the five kittens rushed to her, nestling against her side. "Sir, meet your new babies - five kittens! I had to find a safe place. I had to leave."

The reunion was special. The two cats stared into each other's face then rubbed cheeks purring happily.

"I'm a father! A father – oh wow! You girls leave when you get in a family way... Ye-hoo!" he screamed.

Interrupting him, Puss hissed. "Quiet! You'll scare our babies. Look at this little fellow here; he looks just like you. He has your big blue eyes."

Lil' Red cleared her throat loudly, "Looks like we have another resident! Welcome, Sir. You've already become a part of our heart."

The day was beautiful and inviting. It wasn't easy to stay inside. The puppies and kittens were entertaining the others with their play. A kitten would jump onto a puppy then run only to be chased.

Fluffy panted, "It's hot in here. Can't we go out?"

Dal answered, "We have to stay out of sight. We've come too far. Don't worry, we'll get our thinking caps on and work out a plan for the rest of us."

"If winter comes we—," Fluffy cried. "I'm scared!"

Spike patted her back with his tail. "Come on Fluffy, we'll go out and rest under the house for a while. You know, life is what you make of it. Change only comes with effort. We'll think together."

The two lapped a bit of water and went to the underside of the building.

Lil' Red smiled after they left. "Spike is right. It's time to plan. We all need homes. Tonight, Zipper and Peppie can leave for Rosie's place. The cats will be fine here."

Zipper grinned from ear-to-ear. "Peppie, did you hear that? We can go home tonight! Oh glory! Glory! Glory!"

Peppie jumped up and flopped across her kin-dog. "Rosie keeps her store open real late. After dark, that will be perfect!"

"I want Spike to go with us. When Becky and David come for me, he can go with us," Zipper decided.

"Do you think so? They won't send him to the old dog shelter?" responded Lil' Red.

"Oh, no! Becky is putty in my paws!" Zipper snickered. "We'll leave when the cars are gone. People leave town at night."

"We'll miss you," sobbed Bonnie. "I can't leave my puppies. I don't know what we'll do."

"Let us go to Rosie's. In a couple daylights send somebody to Rosie's place. Maybe we can help out," Peppie whispered. "It makes me feel sort of bad to leave you here. After all, we made a pact. We are a pack."

Lil' Red beamed, "What a great plan. You can be our spy. Check it out and you can act as our adoption agency."

"We should go to Rosie's real late. We have to stay in touch. Everybody needs to know how to find Peppie," Zipper planned. "Somebody needs to walk along."

"That will be great. We can let Dally, Babe, and Collie walk you to Rosie's. They will come back and the rest of us can know how to get to the dress shop in case something happens," Lil' Red suggested.

"Yes! Yes! Yes! That's perfect! I'd love to go there. Rosie will help us just because she loves dogs," Collie agreed. "I know she has to be a dog fanatic!"

Peppie rolled wildly and jumped up. "She'd take everybody if she could. Rosie is our answer!"

Bernie the Saint Bernard yawned. His mouth opened like a monster tiger and his sigh was a near roar. He said, "Something so big as me isn't wanted. I'm still young, but people think I'm mean because of my huge size. They think I hog up tons of food. I may never find a home again."

"We pray something will happen!" Collie consoled and looked at the bushes just outside their entrance. "Hey, look at that!"

Quickly, he rushed to the tree with Babe by his side.

"Nut! That's nothing but a bunch of sticks!' laughed the stately greyhound.

"Look again!" demanded Collie shaking her silky coat into place. "I know about this. See that *stick* has a cute head, wings and great long legs."

"My gosh! They do!" amazed Lil' Red just behind them.

The four-inch long 'sticks' moved around until they were in a line on the fat bush like tree. They seemed friendly as they twitched slightly.

"They are Praying Mantises! See? I'll ask them," Collie informed and turned in the doorway. "Hey Mantises, we have a problem. Our big dog, Bernie, needs a home too. Can you pray for him to find a home?

The largest of the big insects jumped to hang on the side of the doorway. He was not very noisy like lots of insects. He sat staring, checking out the situation. Finally, he said, "Yelp! We'll do that. We usually *prey* instead of 'pray' but we are all God's creatures. We can pray for your big beast."

With a sweeping motion, he urged all the other companion critters onto the pathway by the door. They lined up three wide about two feet long.

One Mantis grinned, "Would you believe we are all one family from one cocoon?"

The dogs stared in disbelief.

The chief Mantis whispered, "Alright, let's pray!"

All the insects snapped into praying position and the dogs and cats followed by sitting into a calm state.

"Please, God," they all prayed --------" Help us find homes! And God, especially bless Bernie – he sure is huge-----"

# Treats & Tales

# Chapter 15

It was quiet in the little city of Sunnydale. There was no traffic. The town square clock bonged eight times. Lil' Red stood with tears in her eyes. She nodded, "Alright - *eight clock bongs* - it's time for the three of you to go home."

Peppie rolled and wiggled, "I'm *happy-sad*."

"You're what?" Lil' Red laughed.

"Well, I'm glad I'm found but sad to leave my friends," Peppie cried. Her little red Chihuahua head showed its apple point as she lifted her brow.

"Sooner or later, we all have to do what we have to do," Zipper reminded them. "Our goal was to run for our lives from the dog pound, then find our homes. The Mantises prayed; we prayed – have faith!"

"Go! Go now! It's time," insisted Lil' Red. She kissed Zipper, Peppie and Spike. "Good luck, we'll miss you."

"Stay in touch with Peppie!" urged Spike.

All the pack and kittens watched them disappear down the path. The three who would go home scampered a half block ahead of the three who would return. Quickly, Peppie, Zipper and Spike turned and rushed back to take a last look at the shed. The dogs and kitties were lined up in a row.

Peppie stood on her back feet and blew a kiss to the group. Then, Zipper and Spike did the same.

Lil' Red smiled, "Throw one back!"

Happily, the crowd bid a final farewell. Fluffy cried, "I'll always remember you! Bye, I love you!"

Again, Spike, Zipper and Peppie raced out of sight. The group at the shed returned to their nightly routine.

It was a fast walk to the fountain area. The six dogs slipped into the shadows to check the city. Zipper whispered, "It looks like we can go on."

"Sh! Sh! Sh!" cautioned Collie. "We'd better play it carefully from here. We can't get caught by the police."

"I know!" Spike sighed and pointed, "Rosie is that way!"

"How far?" asked Babe. "I miss the track sometimes. Maybe it will be a nice run."

"We can't do a lot of running," teased Dally. "Only Greyhounds are fit to run. Right now, we have to stay low; creep and sneak."

"I sure wish I had a chance to run. There is no place for me. I'm real young, five years old. I was in lots of dog races. In my Greyhound group, I was a top winner for a long time. I won ribbons, cups, flowers, trophies, gifts and money. As long as I was on top, my master did all sorts of special things for me. Once I hurt my leg, I was a goner! He gave me to a couple, but they couldn't afford the different shots I needed. They had never had a pet before. You guessed it, when I got sick, they took me to the animal shelter."

"Wow! Another *dump-the-dog* story!" blasted Collie. "People are something else when they throw away their pet."

"I know you think that's bad. Here's what happened to me," Collie recalled. "I was living on a big farm. I helped bring in cows, hogs and sheep. Those big beasts would run over you if you didn't keep your head in the job. I learned to work farm animals at six months with my Pa-Pa dog. It's really a trick and a fun job. I could see how the other dogs there admired me; people praised me constantly."

"Dog-gone, what happened?" Zipper asked.

"Well, one day the people sold their farm. The cows, pigs, chickens, ducks and sheep went to slaughter. They took their cats to the people next door. I was just left there like I didn't exist, totally abandoned," continued Collie, with a faraway look in his eyes.

"They sold the farm?" Peppie squealed. "How awful!"

"I was sad when I found out the people sold the place. The state bought the stuff for making roads. I was left with nobody to care for me. The roads couldn't make a life for me. The big machines came. They pushed down the out-building and barns. Big trucks moved the farmhouse to another place down the highway. Then one day, a sheriff truck came. They put a collar around my neck from a long stick and I was put into that truck. That night, I was put in the Sunnydale Animal Shelter. The good thing, at least I had a good meal and fresh water."

"Oh, Collie, I'm so sorry. That was such a nice life," Babe contributed. "It may not be easy, somehow, we'll find a home."

"Don't hold your breath! We're not so desirable. Think about it – the people who had us just flipped us away as if we were dirty shorts," worried Collie.

"This is the beginning of a new and wonderful life for us all. I promise you that!" grinned Peppie. "I feel it in my bones. We've made it this far."

"That's easy for you girl. You're almost home," replied Babe, choking back the big lump. "I'm happy for you---"

"Well, I'm not there yet. Suppose Rosie has replaced me, what would I do?" Peppie revealed her greatest fear. "We've all been away from our humans for many, many days."

Collie soothed, "Don't get paranoid little Chihuahua. Just calm down, we'll go find Rosie's shop."

"I'm ready!" jumped Zipper squealing. "Let's hit the trail!"

Dally stood tall and shook his strong body. Fine hair filtered through the air. "I feel like I know where we're going. I rode our trucks everywhere. That way? Is that where Rosie is?"

"Cat showed US! Yes! That's it! Follow me!" demanded Spike. "I could find it with my eyes closed."

It was about a ten-minute walk. The six buddies eased down the street. It was like a tomb; nothing stirring, not even a mouse, rat or lizard. Quickly, they could see a building that was fronted with glass. You could see inside if you peeped around the treasures. Here there were strange headless and armless women wearing beautiful gowns. This night, the lights beamed a sea of radiant red that glistened in the breeze from a ceiling fan. The sequins and beads pronounced their distinctive glamour.

The six sat in awe in a row in front of the store. Their jaws dropped; they gasped with excitement. It was the most fantastic vision imaginable.

"This is a dream!" whispered Babe.

"No, this is heaven!" sighed Collie.

"Oh, mercy, it's paradise!" envied Dally. "Just look at it! I love it! Hey, look Peppie! There's somebody in there!"

Peppie began to shiver then the exciting trembling started. "It's Rosie! It's Rosie! It's Rosie!"

"Go on, make a noise, get her to the door! You're home!" urged Babe.

"Wait until Babe, Collie and me hide," directed Dally. "We'll be watching across the street. Good luck Zipper, Peppie and Spike. We'll be in touch!"

The six rubbed cheeks and hips and licked ears. Immediately, three crossed the street and slipped into the shadows.

"Stay with me!" cried Peppie. She stood on the glass door and banged with her tiny feet, but Rosie couldn't hear her.

"Heck with this," Spike snarled. "Let me at the door!"

Spike took his body and slammed against it nearly knocking himself out. The door rattled loudly; Rosie looked up. The three animals stood with their hands on the clear entry. They waited again.

"She can't hear us!" cried Peppie.

Suddenly, Rosie swiftly walked toward them. Then, she started to run. They could hear her moan, "Oh! Goodness! Oh, my! It's my baby! Momma will open the door in a minute!"

Rosie fumbled until the glass between them was pushed open wide. She sat on the entry floor crying, "Peppie! Oh, Peppie! My baby girl! I've missed you so much! I thought you were gone forever!"

Peppie had already jumped into her arms and was licking her wonderful face. She whined and cried and sucked up the pleasure of the reunion. Peppie wished Rosie could understand her animal language, "I'm home! I'm home forever!"

"You beautiful, precious doll! I love you!" Rosie cried real hot human tears. Suddenly, she looked in front of her. "Zipper? Is that you Zipper? Well I'll be doggone! It's Zipper too! Come here honey!"

"Rosie! Grandma! I'm here! I love you!" Zipper exclaimed as he rushed into her arms and showered her with a smoldering tongue licking around her eyes and ears.

"Zip you little rascal. Where have you been? Wait until Becky and David hear about this. Better still I'm taking you to them now!" Rosie promised. "They will absolutely die!"

Zipper jumped down and urged Spike to Rosie. "Shake her hand Spike!"

The dog sat and held his hand for Rosie to grasp carefully. He whined and smiled trying to tell her he was glad to meet her.

Peppie moaned, "Spike, roll over! She loves that!"

The big white dog dropped to the floor and slipped onto his back with a wide toothy smile.

Rosie grinned, "Come here, handsome! We'll find a place for you too. I have a feeling you've been watching after my babies."

Rosie brought the three inside and took them to the familiar kitchen where Peppie and Zipper had loved to stay. She placed three bowls of water on the floor and the animals lapped a generous amount.

"Hungry?" she asked. "Let me check the freezer."

The George Foreman cooker was quickly grilling three nice Porterhouse steaks. While they cooked, Rosie went into her cabinet and set three beautiful placemats in a row. The three happy dogs sat watching. Finally, she placed a steak on beautiful white china then poured milk in champagne crystal glasses.

"The steak is a bit hot. I'll cut them up!" She smiled and made them into pieces. Once done she whispered, "Let's pray. Peppie, do you remember this?"

Peppie rolled over and placed her hands together Zipper and Spike followed, doing the same.

Rosie closed her eyes, "Thank you God for bringing our babies home. Bless them. Bless their food! Amen."

The rare steak was almost breathtaking. The three enjoyed their first dinner home. Rosie called her daughter, "You have to come here. It's an emergency!"

They made an agreement and soon Becky and David rushed into the back door. Becky yelled, "What's the emergency?"

David smiled, "Is that Zipper?"

Becky went crazy, "Little man! You're home! Oh what happened to you? Where did he come from?"

Once more there were tears, kissing and hugging. Everyone was crazy with happiness.

"Well, Zipper and Peppie are back, but look what came with them!" laughed Rosie.

"Oh! He's beautiful!" Becky cautiously squealed.

"He's big! I like a big dog!" David assured them. "We could take him with us. You don't have enough space here."

"Good! He's ours Mother!" agreed Becky.

Spike slipped gently into Becky's lap and rubbed his head against her cheeks. He was saying with a whimper, "Thank you, I'll be wonderful, just like Zipper, even better."

The reunion was perfect. Zipper and Spike jumped into the backseat of the beautiful BMW. Peppie left with Rosie to cuddle to her back in the soft pillows and feather comforter.

Collie, Dally and Babe watched them leave.

"This mission is complete. They're home! Home sweet home. Let's go back and report," Collie sat staring at the beautiful window. "I'm happy for them!"

The three hurried to the shack with the superb news and happy details.

# Chapter 16

It had been about a week since Collie, Dally and Babe had returned from delivering Zipper, Peppie, and Spike to their homes. Although the group still left at the shed was happy for the three; they missed them.

"Wonder what Peppie is doing!" exclaimed Fluffy. "I'll bet they are living high!"

"Of course they are," Collie appraised. "We were across the street watching. Rosie went ballistic. She was so happy. I would about die to have a human love me like that. Some people just touch, kiss and pet their dog. She's like that."

Babe smiled, "My silly bones could sure take some of that soft rubbing. When are we going back to check on Peppie? She can't come to us. Rosie will never let her go."

"That's a *true-ism*!" yielded Dally. "You know; I was thinking we need to go visit Peppie. Rosie will let her go out to *potty* then we could see her."

"Yes, but that would be daytime," reminded Collie.

"I'll chance it," smiled Dally. "Rosie won't send us to a dog shelter. She'd help us find something. I'll bet she'd be able to get me to the firehouse."

"That's probably true!" Fluffy wagged her tail "What about the rest of us? Living in this shed all dirty and eating scraps isn't good. It's getting colder at night too."

Lil' Red stared in space, "I'll never see Mumsie again. Her son hated me. He hated all dogs. Many times he would kick me around until I'd fly under the bed and hide. He was mean to Mumsie too. Once he got her sent away, all of her stuff became his."

"People! Some are so greedy; they'd sell their soul!" Babe consoled. "They say dogs don't have souls, but then we might. I believe you'll find Mumsie. Love is strong. Cross your toes and believe."

Lil' Red smiled, "Alright, we have to remember the good things that already happened to us. Go check on Peppie."

"I will," Dally nodded. "Cat, you want to play detective?"

The big white male feline stood with a hunched back. "Us together? What an odd couple we'd be."

"For this trip, it will be perfect. Your motor can rattle its way into that store with Peppie. Rosie knows you. You're our best spy," urged Dally.

"Well, I am terrific!" Cat boasted. "Let's go, that is if Puss will be alright."

"Go!" smiled Puss.

The two rushed out the doorway. Birds were chirping and jumping around the bushes. Cat hissed, "I might get Puss one of them when we return."

"A bird? A feathered raw bird?" scoffed Dally. "How could you eat that?"

"Wait up!" growled Mark running in their direction. He stopped between the two and shook his beautiful coat. "Wow! I itch! I had to get out of there. I hope I don't have a flea. You know it's easy to pass them around in a group. We need to get a box of that powder stuff to put in the shed."

"I suppose. We could have worms, bugs, and kennel diseases, all sorts of things. We need homes soon!" Dally explained.

"I'll bet Peppie can get us medicines from Rosie. Cat, you can go inside there, can't you?" inquired Mark.

"Sure, Rosie lets me come and go," the white cat purred. He was very vain and tried to keep his coat perfect. "Rosie will brush me if I make a fuss over her."

"Here's the fountain park. Maybe we'd better separate to cross the street," Mark suggested.

"Five minutes and we'll meet behind the store," insisted Dally.

It was a smooth move. Quickly, the three were sitting in the bushes by the dress shop. "Listen!" Cat thumped his foot. "Stay down."

The back door opened, "Come on Peppie! Potty! Now is the perfect time before things get busy."

Soon, Peppie happily ran beside the store. She could smell a familiar scent. She barked gently, "Woof! Woof!" walking around and sniffing was her early morning activity.

Cat hissed, "Sisss! Peppie!"

The dog followed the sound. Cat emerged with a smile and ran to Rosie. He flipped his tail and wrapped it around Rosie's legs.

She bent down and picked him up. Happily, she kissed his big head, "Cat! Where have you been? I've missed you! Peppie's home too!"

Reluctantly, Dally stood. His spotted white coat was unmistakably Dalmatian. He stared at Rosie; she stared back in disbelief. "My Lord, it's the Firehouse Dog! Easy boy, I won't hurt you! Peppie bring him here!"

Cat winked at Dally with a grin and in cat words spoke, "Yeah — she wants you too! Go on and let her touch you."

Rosie reached down and patted the smiling dog. "You are beautiful! When Peppie gets finished we'll go inside. I was just getting ready to cook breakfast for Peppie."

Peppie sniffed a little more and completed her yard break. She had discovered Mark was with them. She barked again and told Mark to follow. While Rosie held the door, Cat and all the dogs followed Peppie inside.

Rosie stepped in and stared at the handsome, perfectly marked stately German Shepherd. "Oh well, where did you come from fellow? Well, what the heck, it's only one more dish on the floor. You folks need some special care. Eat first. I have a couple hours before work.'

She poured Cat a nice bowl of milk and gave each dog a bowl of water. Each enjoyed the clean bug-free liquid.

Peppie smiled, "Do you believe in heaven now?"

"This is it for certain," winked Dally as he watched Rosie open the refrigerator. His heart began to pound and his lips filled with water. Drooling, he watched her open a large package of bacon and flip it onto a pan. The aroma was another piece of heaven.

Cat, Dally, Mark and Peppie sat quietly. A buzz broke the silence. The woman picked up one of those little boxes that all humans carry around. She said, "Hi, it's Rosie!"

They heard mumbles from the 'box'. She cleared her throat, "Oh yes, well I'd love to. I haven't seen you in a long time. How about tomorrow afternoon?"

The dogs cocked their heads listening to Rosie. "Guess what? I'm doing a little fashion show at the Sunnydale Nursing Care. I've wanted to do that for so long. Older people need to be in touch with the real world! Sometimes, they buy things from me too!"

Peppie whined, "Got that? The *nursing home*; somebody go tell Lil' Red. Maybe we can find Mumsie for her!"

The bacon was placed on four paper plates in front of each. Cat laughed, "This is alright, but a nice fresh mouse would be a real delicacy!"

"Uck! Mouse! This is heaven!" Dally chomped down on one beautiful piece. He licked his lips and grinned, "Peppie, are there any mice here? Maybe I could trade him bacon for one."

"Of course not, you know humans - keep it clean"

They finished the food then gathered around Peppie's bowl overflowing with crunch-mix. "This is good too!" Dally guzzled.

"Eat all you want. She keeps this full," Peppie insisted. "As soon as that door opens, get out of here, go to the shack and tell Red everything. Somebody needs to follow us tomorrow."

Things didn't go as they expected. Rosie closed off the inside doors and left them in the *in-house dog run*. This frightened them.

"I can climb over," Cat reminded.

"It will be all right, don't worry!" assured Peppie, "We can sleep awhile." She rolled onto her back with her front paws extended.

Later, Rosie returned with a happy heart, "I've got a surprise for you!" She got on her knees and patted Dally. "You are a sweet handsome prince!"

Someone gently pecked on the door, and then entered. Looking up, the animals observed a tall uniformed man. Dally recognized him and jumped into his arms.

The man gasped, "Dally! Oh my ole buddy! Come here! I'm taking you home! Boy how we've missed you!"

Dally licked every inch of his face. He was happy to see the Captain. This was an answer to his world. "Home? The firehouse?" he was conveying in dog language. Trembling was always his persuading power.

"Yes, Dally you can come to the firehouse when I work. My wife wants you at our house when I'm off duty," the frrefighter smiled and petted all the critters.

Soon, he hooked a leash to Dally. The two walked out the door. Dally looked at his friends smiling back. He was home – he was found.

Peppie cried, "Wasn't that beautiful? I'll bet Rosie knows we need to get out. Once that door opens, hurry outside. Go back, tell Red. I'll ride with Rosie to the fashion show. I can remember how to get to the place."

Rosie had been in another room talking to humans. She rushed back, "Sorry, babies, hope you found enough to eat."

Mark wanted to have her pack a basket but knew it wouldn't happen.

Peppie whined and put her foot to the door three times. She was smiling.

"Oh! I'm sorry. You need to go out!" apologized Rosie over and over, and then opened the door. "I'll be right out; I need my coat."

Mark and Cat bound happily out of sight before looking back to see Peppie wave goodbye. Her bottom teeth glistened like little pearls from her happy smile.

The phone was ringing off the hook. Rosie told the critters to come inside when they were finished. Racing to catch the call she made it in time. "It's Rosie!"

"No kidding!" laughed the party calling.

"Gale! I was going to talk to you today. You'll never believe it. My baby is back!"

"You mean Peppie?" she cried.

"Yes! Peppie just appeared in front of the store. It's unreal!" gleed Rosie. "I had actually given up."

"Wonder who stole her?" asked Gale.

"We'll never really know!" replied Rosie.

"Put her on the phone!" insisted Gale.

"Peppie, your Aunt Gale is on the phone. Here, talk to her. Listen!" She put the phone to her dogs' ear; Peppie listened.

"Peppie! Hello sweetie! This is Aunt Gale. Are you all right? We're sure happy you are home." As the woman talked the dog grinned and listened and whined hearing her voice. Finally, Peppie barked lightly, in dog language she said, "Aunt Gale, I can't wait for you to come to see me. I'd love some Georgia peaches in milk!"

Gale whispered, "I'll bring my baby some peaches!"

Finally, Rosie and Gale completed their call.

Rosie said to Peppie, "Aunt Gale is coming to give you a welcome home party. We'll invite everybody! "

Peppie smiled, "You don't know the half of it; this party will be real peachy.

# Chapter 17

Cat was hanging angrily in a tree several blocks from their shed. He was hissing and screaming, "You jerk - get away from here! Yeah! I said get outta here. Go-ooo-ooo! Gooooo-ooo!"

Mark was standing beside a trashcan. He was laughing.

"Yeah – yeah! You like this? Yeah!" hissed Cat.

Mark waltzed to the classy-looking female Weimaraner. She was barking at the base of the tree. With his approach, she settled down.

Mark smiled and winked, "Are you from here?" He could see a broken chain hanging from her neck.

"My house is over there," she pointed and flipped her eyelids flirtatiously. "Sugar-pie, I don't remember seeing you before."

Spike whispered, "Let the cat get down. We are on our way home. "

"You live with a feline? Aren't you nervous?"

"No, he's a buddy. Take a walk with me. A cat's not such a great toy. They can be right handy. What do you say beautiful? How about us making some music together?" Mark urged and nodded for Cat to get down.

Cat dropped from the tree to run home. Mark and the silky dog stood bumping heads, licking ears and caressing.

Cat didn't stop until he was able to fly inside the 'shed'. He grumbled, "Mark is nuts! Is everybody in here all right? Where are my kittens and Puss?"

The little kitties and puppies wiggled all over him with a happy welcome.

"Where's Dally and Mark?" prodded Lil' Red. "It's late. We've been worried. You should have come back sooner."

"Good news – bad news!" the white animal sighed.

"Really?" Fluffy began a flow of tears and cried, "They're dead? Caught by the animal shelter? Lost? What? Tell us! We know Peppie has to be alright!"

Lil' Red looked through the open door, "Where are they?"

"The good news first." Cat began, "Dally got to go back to the fire department. Rosie knows everything. One call to the fire station and Dally was home! His partner picked him up."

"Then what?" asked Terry, the rat terrier.

"We ate like kings before the call on that talking box," Cat sneezed. "Where's my pretty Puss?"

"Up here!" the partner cat answered. She was brushing her hair with her tongue. Cat climbed and jumped to join her.

A huge noise from outside concerned the group. Soon, they realized it was Mark with a strange dog. Lil' Red sighed, "My gosh! Why is he bringing another dog here? We're trying to get away not multiply!"

Outside the door, they could see him playing and chasing around with the sleek Weimaraner. Lil' Red had to admire his taste. The others stared in amazement.

Mark rolled with the brownish-grey creature, "I'll be back." He stuck his head in the air sniffing.

"Mark! I was concerned, but I understand," smiled Lil' Red. "Cat was crazy with worry when he came back."

"Oh, cats! My friend chased him; you know cats! They live nervous. Look at that beautiful girl! She just wanted to play. Everything' s cool!"

"Let me warn you, if that dog goes missing, her folks will set the world on fire finding her. You'd better send her home! Besides, we don't need you to be stupid and drag pups in. A female that size will have 8 to 12 puppies," warned Red.

"Dummy, we're just pals. She can't have babies. As they say, she's *fixed!*" Mark added. "I just thought she was pretty!"

"Thank God!" breathed Fluffy openly. "It's wonderful Dal went home. Peppie has to be happy."

"Like a bug in a rug! Best news of all is yet to be told," grinned the handsome German Shepherd. "Cat is such an air-head, he should have told you this first."

"What? Told what," Lil' Red flipped.

"Sit down, you'll faint! Rosie and Peppie are going to a *nursing home* tomorrow to do a fashion show!" Mark smiled sparkling with pride. "I think we have found your Mumsie!"

Suddenly, there was a loud thump. All eyes turned to see Lil' Red who always tried to be tough, stretched out on the floor.

"Oh my gosh! Red fainted!" whispered Bonnie with a puppy nursing her.

"I'll handle this!" rumbled Bernie. He stood and his huge Saint Bernard jowls flibbered from side to side. He pushed her motionless body around then began puffing into her nostrils.

Immediately, Red came around. She opened her eyes and smiled, "Uck! I thought I was in a tunnel when I woke up looking down that big throat!"

"Are you alright?" Terry pleaded as he touched her head.

"I'm in shock!" Lil' Red breathed, "Mumsie? How could she be here?"

"That's possible!" Mark assured. "Peppie is going to find out how to get to the nursing home then----."

"Oh no! We'll follow them there?" interrupted Red.

"We can't keep up with a car!" Terry reasoned. "Besides, can't you see a bunch of dogs chasing a car in the middle of town?"

Mark spoke softly, "Lil' Red, you have to let us help you. I'm going. I'll work it out. Trust me! I've tried to be everybody's big brother. Now, it's your turn for me to *brother* you."

Red gasped, then her big brown eyes filled with joy. "You're right, Mark. If anyone can create this miracle, it will be you. Please find my Mumsie!"

"Just leave it to me. See that our group is ready for a big change. If you leave us, it will be rough. We depend on you," he told her.

"That's nice but sad. Our goal is to find a home for each of us. If I find Mumsie, I promise I will not forget any of you," swore Lil' Red.

Bonnie gave a low growl. Quickly, the five kittens and five puppies raced toward her playful call. At her feet, they rolled and played with each other. Bonnie laughed, "They are almost ready to leave the nest."

"That's what's so sad," whimpered Red. "They have become such friends and now we're going to go in different directions. It has to happen. Bonnie don't have anymore puppies!"

"I don't need to, but I'm just a plain old beagle. When we go into that heat, things happen. Fools come from everywhere and gang up on you. It's hard to hide," sniffed the black and tan mother.

"If Mark finds Mumsie, I may leave. Suppose, she is in a place that won't take me," Red worried.

"Hey look! There's those Praying Mantises!" Bonnie scampered to the doorway. "Hey, insects! Please say a prayer for our friend Lil' Red. She wants to go home to Mumsie. We need homes, each one of us."

The huge daddy bug smiled and shook his head up and down. He lifted his right leg and fluttered a long spindly wing. Even more mantises appeared in front of the shack. They settled together upholding a praying position. Everything was silent as they quietly went through what seemed like a sacred ceremony. Several minutes later, they swarmed to a nearby bush.

"I feel better. Humans pray every time they get into trouble. I sure wish we could each have our own Mantis with us all the time," Bonnie said. "I'm going to pray for my babies to find a home. It will be awful to lose them."

Bonnie began to cry. Fluffy rushed to her and gathered her brown and tan head against her small white curly body. "We will be alright. Don't cry Bonnie! It is already working. Peppie will help us too."

The pack of dogs agreed to become more serious about their future. "Wishing, dreaming and praying is our future," grinned Cat. "We are alive!"

"Yeah, alive and outside looking in," worried Babe.

Bernie grunted, "When my big head finds a home the world will turn red!"

"There's always a place for everyone. Maybe we'd better find Bernie a home first. He'll be hardest to place," Lil' Red scratched an ear. "You need a farm I suppose."

They continued to worry until the next day. Mark walked to the top of the hill, and then waved. Again, out of sight he ran in the shadows to the fountain. With the town quiet, he raced to a bush beside Rosie's place. He was tired and fell asleep.

# Chapter 18

A loud rumble startled Mark. He awakened to a door slamming and scratching nearby. Through one eye, he watched Peppie taking her early morning 'bout. He cleared his throat then yawned. Peppie looked up.

From a distance, Rosie was calling, "Peppie! Peppie!"

"Come on, Mark. Eat breakfast with me!" Peppie smiled. "It'll be alright!"

"I don't know. That gang at the shack is getting restless and Bernard is a special concern and the ten baby kitties and pups are ready to go too. If Red leaves, everything will fall apart," replied the fine German Shepherd.

"We have to check out that old-peoples' place for Red. She has done so much for all of us. It wouldn't be fair," reminded Peppie. "A promise is a promise."

"The truth, Lil' Red sure is bossy!"

"So? Somebody had to be boss. Where would we be?" Peppie defended her friend. "Come on, Rosie knows you now."

Rosie spotted Peppie with Mark. "Hey! Come here fellow. Come inside Peppie; bring your friend. I wonder where he lives. Poor fellow, you're terribly skinny. Somebody would love to make you their pet. We'll work on that."

Once more, inside Rosie's place was a dream-treat. Her kitchen smelled like the best food possible. Mark's eyes rolled with excitement. He appeared calm on the outside although drooling from the odors.

Rosie placed a large plate before him. He stared in disbelief; bacon, eggs and oatmeal. Peppie had the same thing but a smaller amount. At once, the two again began to eat. Soon, both plates were empty. Rosie gave them a bowl of milk each.

"We've got to hurry Peppie. The people will think we're not coming. I must put these things in the car. Becky and her friend are meeting us there," Rosie informed.

Mark laughed, "I love to hear her talk to you like you're a person."

Peppie winked, "Listen, that's Becky coming in!"

The back door flew open. The pretty woman slipped inside. She squatted and tossed the hair on the neck of both dogs. "Hello, Peppie! Your friend, Zipper is in the car. Well – who do we have here?"

Mark smiled showing his teeth and wagging his tail. Becky hugged him gently, "I think you need a home too! Mother, where did you get this dog?"

"He just shows up to see Peppie. I feel sorry for him being on the street. We need to get him placed. Poor fellow, he's too thin," Rosie informed. "Feel his ribs."

"We'd better hurry and leave. Lisa is modeling with me. She loves all animals and I know she'll take this fella with her," Becky said. "Can Peppie ride with Zipper and me?"

"Well, maybe. We'll both drive. Big boy, you can come along," Rosie offered. Mark flipped on his back onto the floor with Peppie. The two were expressing their approval. Becky rubbed their tummies, "Oh goodness! You two are spoiled!"

It was a short drive to the Sunnydale Retirement Center. Mark was belted in the seat beside Rosie. He watched every inch of the trip to be able later to find the retirement place. In fact, he felt so great he thought, 'I wish I had a cigar; it would be a perfect touch. I'm debonair!'

Becky parked next to Rosie. When she caught a glimpse of Mark in his seat belt, she laughed. "Mother! You're a trip! The big dog looks like a person there."

"Hurry," urged Rosie grabbing a huge sheet filled with garments. They have a security check here. We'll have to leave these dogs out here."

"Here's Lisa!" she waved to the girl parking her vehicle. "I'm taking Zipper with me. My pet carrier is a purse; nobody will know."

Together, they entered the reception area. A tall darkhaired sophisticated lady stood extending her hand "You must be Rosie! Our residents are already in the solarium. They are so excited."

"Show us where to go. The girls need a place to change. They'll wear eight outfits each."

Quickly, details fell into place. Rosie was introduced. The show started with a French CD and a smile.

"Ladies and Gentlemen – straight from Paris and New York, we'll bring you the newest look of the season!"

"We need to see the new pajamas and bathrobes!" snickered a frail man in a wheelchair.

"Hush, Elmer! Go to your room if you can't behave!" a lady warned.

The Director who had met Rosie earlier cautioned, "Shish!"

"Shish – shish – shish!" barked the man. "Why don't you bring a car show or something? Always, entertainment is for the girls."

"Elmer, just enjoy yourself You ought to like seeing pretty women. You ain't that old!" grinned another small man.

Elmer winked and resigned, "Oh, pretty girls? Well bring them on!"

Everyone laughed. They relaxed to watch the two beautiful young women walk the designated path of fashion. It only took a half-hour to win their applause that begged for more.

Elmer blurted out, "Yeah! Can't we see it again?"

Rosie was completing the finale with the two girls together displaying jogging suits in a soft satin. This brought total excitement as they slipped off the matched long-sleeved jacket to reveal a simple hip-length over shirt.

A whistle from Elmer brought laughter.

Rosie smiled, "Especially for Elmer. Girls give him your best!"

Quickly, Becky and Lisa stepped out of the long pants to reveal matching shorts; then, a flip of the shirt; they were sporting a strappy waist-cut top. A little revealing, but useful.

All the residents were thrilled. When the models left the staging area, the huge applause brought them back.

Becky and Lisa stood smiling, enjoying the clapping and whistles. The applause quickened and laughter surmounted. They looked at each other then down.

"Oh no! I'm in trouble!" whispered Becky. "How'd she get in here?"

Lisa smiled as she spoke through her teeth, "I brought her."

On the floor in front of them lay Zipper and Peppie sucking up the attention of applause and laughter. Both chose to flop onto their backs and wait.

Rosie smiled through her embarrassment. "You can always match a nice play suit to your pet. Here Zipper is wearing a casual leather bib and Peppie is displaying the sleeveless satin body shirt. Note her pretty bows and nail polish!"

Becky and Lisa picked up the animals presenting a loving touch as a final finale. The residents had experienced the most exciting program ever.

"Zipper!" scolded Becky. "You were supposed to stay hidden. You've got mother in trouble."

Peppie growled, "Who cares! They loved us!"

Zipper panted and grinned, "We're the stars!"

The after-show excitement was the greatest. A table of special treats was lavishly served. Everyone gathered around, selecting their portions. Lisa and Becky had slipped back into their long pants and shirts to mingle.

Elmer whistled gently, "Here puppy!"

Both dogs wiggled from the arms of the models and rushed to him for the big hunks of strawberry cake and glasses of milk the man had placed on the floor. Instantly, they looked at each other and consumed it all to the final lapping of the plate.

A very nice lady walked over to the dogs. "Can I hold your Dachshund?" she whispered with tears in her eyes.

Becky smiled, "Well, of course. Zipper, this lady wants to pet you. And what is your name?"

"Mumsie," she trembled as she held Zipper to her face. "Oh you feel so sweet! My name is Mumsie!"

Zipper relaxed and enjoyed her scratching him under his throat. His leg kept wiggling from the touch.

Peppie observed, "She's nice! This is Mumsie!"

The woman continued, "Before I came here to live, I had a wonderful little Dachshund. Her name was Little Red. I miss her so much. My son gave her away. I think of her every night. I pray that she's all right and has a home. But I know, she was dumped at the animal shelter. She might be dead."

Mumsie broke into heavy weeping, laying her head on Zipper's neck. Becky caressed her shoulders. "I'm sorry to bring back sad memories."

"Oh no, I have good memories of Lil' Red; I just miss her!" Mumsie cried.

Peppie told Zipper, "We found Mumsie!"

Rosie, Becky and Lisa gathered all their show items and left for the store. When they arrived, the three dogs gathered around the water bowl. Peppie flipped her pointed ears, "Mark, we met Mumsie; she was there crying over Lil' Red. We found her!"

Zipper chuckled, "Yeah, she was nuts about me! Held me, scratched and kissed me! It was embarrassing!"

"Really? You loved it!" Peppie exclaimed.

"If I can get out of here, I'll tell Red," Mark sadly replied. "It's all coming to an end."

"Don't worry," Peppie consoled. "We're all going home. Home is what we need. It's not an end; it's a beginning. I'm happy; Zipper is happy. Lisa will take you when you come back. You have to help Lil' Red."

"I understand," Mark's eyes filled with tears.

Once Rosie let them outside to *potty*, Mark bid his goodbyes and trudged toward the fountain.

"Mark is sweet. He is in love with Lil' Red. He doesn't want to lose her!" observed Zipper.

"It will all be all right! I feel it in my bones!" Peppie assured.

"Bones? Which ones? Those in your body or the ones on your plate?" Zipper giggled.

# Chapter 19

"Yuk! You are grosser than gross! Ugh! Drop it!" screamed Lil' Red.

The little white poodle ran into a little grassy area to hide. She was embarrassed.

"Dunce! You silly dunce! Put that down! Now!" roared Bernie. His huge head dropped to stare at the small beast.

Catching his eyes squinting a serious command, Fluffy lay on the green-carpeted turf and reluctantly dropped the long hard object.

"You filthy nut! Poop-breath! Do you think anyone wants a dog that eats *fanny logs*?" yelled Lil' Red. "Shame!"

Fluffy put her head down, "It's dried. I didn't know it was a bad thing."

"Well, it is! Next thing, you'll get sick!" harped Bernie.

"It never made me sick before!" defended Fluffy.

"Maybe not, but the rule is: No poop eating! You got it?" Red insisted.

Fluffy covered her tearing eyes with her paws. "I just didn't think."

"Keep in mind that worms can kill a dog. There's all kinds of awful worms that can get into your body. They can make you real sick too. When one dog has worms or a disease it often passes out the body in the poop. Mumsie used to wash my feet when I'd come in from outdoors so I wouldn't lick bad stuff from them," Lil' Red preached. "You have to be careful. Besides, it'll give you poop-breath."

"Don't tell the others you caught me. I'll never do it again!" Fluffy begged.

Lil' Red snapped her head up and watched the German Shepherd rushing toward her. He was barking happily; then stopped in front of the red dachshund. "Come inside!"

They could see his wet coat and a twinkle in his eye. Red announced, "Inside? Now!"

The pack hurried to listen to Mark reveal his news. The anticipation made them quiver with hope, yet fear. They each thought, what will happen now? Did he find Mumsie?

Fluffy cried, "Oh God! Please don't let Lil' Red leave us. Call in the Praying Mantis!"

Mark smiled showing his teeth, "Yes!" I have found Mumsie! We need a plan! We can't let Lil' Red leave us. We could go with her."

"Let's make a plan to include everyone!" Lil' Red whispered. "I can't ever leave you either."

"Oh yes, call in the Praying Mantises or we are doomed!" yelled Babe. "It will take a move of heaven and earth to solve our needs!"

Fluffy whimpered, "I'm going to the fountain and take a bath. I can look real pretty. Somebody will need a cute little French Poodle like me."

"Bonnie sighed, "I just can't get rid of these five 'blessings'. They are the most beautiful litter in the world. Come to mommie!"

The spunky little puppies lovingly gathered to their mother. Across the room, Puss and her babies were sleeping. Suddenly, one pup rushed from his mother and jumped into the pile of kittens. They jumped with glee, piling on top of a little bulky dog. Their fragile tiny bodies playfully sat on him trying to hold him in place. He squealed and wiggled.

Puss laughed, "The way you do this is hiss, arch your back and throw your paw out like a spider. Like this!"

They watched her as the puppy cried in fear and rolled onto his back. He broke into a near howl. Sweat and tears filled his tiny eyes.

Quickly, Puss pulled him close apologizing, "I'm sorry little baby. I was just teaching the kitties. I wouldn't hurt you for the world." She licked him gently around his ears until he relaxed and stopped shaking.

Bonnie called to him, "The game is over. You see not all cats are friendly. You need to realize that. Their claws can be very sharp. When they scratch, you know it! I've had the blood drawn from them many times!"

Terry wiggled his tail and extended his backside, "See that? I got caught in a corner with a dumb cat at the pound. It still hurts. The pound cops didn't even notice. I thought of grabbing the devil cat behind its neck and shaking its head off."

The puppies looked at the big wide scratch across the side of his thigh. Their mouths dropped in amazement. They backed up to their mother once more trembling. One growled, "Cat – bad cat!"

Fluffy looked carefully. "That's awful. You can get well. I heard if you rub a sore, wart or mole with a rotten dish-rag then bury it under the back steps during a full moon, within a few days it will disappear."

"Do you think so?" Terry asked. "This is deep."

"You can try it. People do it all the time. They're always having warts especially. The moon is full now so, time is right," analyzed Fluffy.

"Where in the world would you find a rotten dish rag?" asked Bernie.

"Mark pointed, "At that hotel, that kitchen. They use rags all the time. They're too lazy to clean them. The things will stink like a skunk. I can slip in there if there's not one in the dumpster."

"Can I go with you?" begged Fluffy. "It was my idea."

"You're too fragile. We must be careful and not be seen outside. I'll take you for a bath at the fountain when I return," Mark promised. "Everyone needs to stay in and be very quiet now."

Soon, Mark hustled out. The dumpster proved to not have the *coveted dish-rag*. Carefully, he crouched down to go beneath the wire fence then dashed to the back door that was partially open.

"Cross your toes!" whispered Fluffy. "He's inside! Oh please don't get caught!"

The animals closed their eyes and prayed, "Oh please come back, Mark!"

When they opened their eyes, they watched Mark running around the inside of the fence. A huge man was chasing him with a long-handled mop. Mark expertly zigged when the man plopped the big weapon just beside him. He zagged quickly to slip through the hole in the fence.

"Bring that bar mop back here you beast!" he yelled. It was too late; "Mark was hiding beside the dumpster. Everyone watched the old man sling the mop in a hissy fit screaming, "If I get my hands on you, I'll beat you to a pulp! You scumbag, flea eaten beast! I'll get you! What 'ja need a rag for is beyond me!"

Mark grinned happily when the man returned inside the hotel. He rejoiced to the others, "I got it!"

At his feet was a filthy half-wet rag. It looked as if it had been through a war then run over by a tractor-trailer. Fluffy gawked, "Oh gee! This is perfectly crusty! Rub it on your sore place, Terry!"

Lil' Red picked up the awful dish-rag and gently massaged the huge deep scratch, "Poor little Terry, you will be alright. Mark has you all fixed up now! Here bury this thing."

"Me? I have to bury it?" Terry asked.

"You sure do! Ain't it your situation?" Lil' Red asked. "Anybody else need healing? Got bumps, warts or spots?"

Several others revealed imperfections and rubbed with the repulsive rag. Being *healed*, they left to bury the rag by the full moon under the steps.

"Well, that's done!" laughed Red, after they returned with earth covered noses and dirty front feet. "People take animals to the veterinarian. They don't resort to witchcraft and tomfoolery. Regular medicine is always best. It's fun too."

"Fun? I'm scared of dog doctors!" Fluffy squeaked and scratched her ear.

"Well, you probably have fleas or mites now. Look at you, scratching all the time. Could be anything!" Red scorned. "Tonight, we'll go to the fountain and take a good bath, kitties, puppies, everybody! We've got to look beautiful. Cat and Puss, that means you too!"

"What kind of 'plan' do you have?" asked Bernie.

Lil' Red winked, "The best ever – trust me!"

Mark rubbed Lil' Red with his head. He felt a lump in his throat. She returned the touch. He whispered, "You are my dream. I love you. I want you back with Mumsie where you'll be happy. I'll be nearby watching. Just know I'll always be here for you."

The two found each other's noses then sniffed gently. Red smiled, "I love you too Mark. You're top dog with me. We all have a forever plan."

Fluffy squalled, "That's beautiful!"

"Come to the fountain," Red directed. "We must get ready. Tomorrow will be the end."

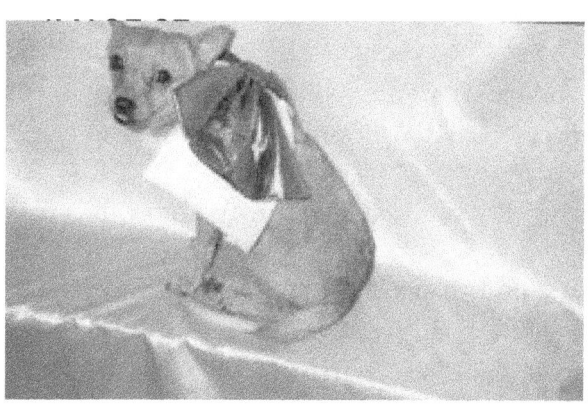

# Chapter 20

"I don't think it can work," cried Fluffy.

"Look!" Lil' Red smiled. "See that pretty face in the water. The reflection is you. Now, who could resist a sweet face like that?"

Terry grinned with an approval of himself as well, "Nobody!"

"We sure do clean up well," grunted Bernie shaking his masterful two-hundred-pound body. "I'm almost dry!"

Lil' Red stood back and observed the others. Babe was sleek and trim; Bonnie and puppies were soft; Puss, Cat, and kittens were all reluctantly in clean and fine condition.

Lil' Red stared and stood, "My Lord, who are you?"

A new dog had joined their pack. She was the tiniest collie dog they had ever seen. When they took their bath at the fountain, she apparently joined them.

The little creature was beautiful and spectacular. She crawled across the ground to Red. "Please, I'm alone. I don't have anybody. I joined in last night hoping you'd help me. I won't cause any trouble," she blubbered.

"I guess we can show her around and leave her here with the shed. There's food and water," stated Terry.

"No, she'll go with us. One more won't make any difference. We win or lose together," Lil' Red demanded.

"Oh, thank you. I'll do anything you say," promised the little new face.

"What's the plan, Lil' Red?" asked Bernie.

"Well, it's real early now. Today, we'll eat; have water and milk Mark brought in last night. At the end of the day we'll leave here and go to the Sunnydale Retirement Center. Mark knows the way. We're going to march in like the 'Million-man March' in Washington, D.C. As a group, we will be important. Individually, you're nothing," Lil' Red shouted.

"That's right! I know the way," shrugged Mark feeling so very important. His eyes sparkled with excitement, "Lil' Red is right. We're all going home. You will follow me!"

The day passed slowly. The animals felt edgy. Terry screamed out, "Get off my tail!"

"Well, wrap it around your butt out of the way or get it cut off like a bulldog!" yelled Babe. "Just keep your dumb tail to yourself!"

"Stop it! Fussing is childish!" Bernie intervened. "There's the Praying Mantises. They've come to pray with us. Come on everybody, let's say our prayers."

"Please, Mantises. Come to the old-folks home with us," begged Fluffy. "We need you."

Lil' Red invited, "She's right. Follow us. There will be a good life for you too at Sunnydale."

"Oh yes," supplied Mark. "The gardens are beautiful there. I know with the water sprinklers and beautiful plants it would be a super retirement for many of you. Just fly over us tonight!"

The head mantis shook his head up and down. He seemed to be a lighter color than most of the others. 'Could he have turned grey with age? That's one for the books,' thought Lil' Red.

After their prayers, Lil' Red and Mark stood. Red smiled, "You know I love each of you. I hope our plan will work out for us. We have to act perfect. There will be no barking, no fighting, no peeing or pooping indoors. There will be no hogging up food, water or milk. We must show good manners. Sit when told. When in doubt, roll over on your back and grin. Stay clean. Roll your eyes a lot and tremble. That's what makes people go crazy! You must promise!"

The animals took the oath of honor and said with raised paws, "We will, we promise."

Cat injected, "It's sort of hard for a cat to follow dog rules. We'll modify our behavior. It's that trembling thing that blows my mind."

Lil' Red laughed, "Let's go. Just remember how to get back here. If things don't work out on the other end, run like a horse and return here. At least you'll be safe."

With their plan of hope, the group marched in a line behind Mark who acted as their guide. He stopped nodding, "Pick up these babies and carry them. We can make better time. They want to scamper around playing."

Bernie flattened to the ground grunting, "Here, kitty, kitty!"

Puss pushed the five kittens on top Bernie's soft bed of a coat. The kitties clung to him as he stood. Bernie took one puppy by his neck. The other four were carried by Bonnie, Babe, Terry and the new little collie.

"Can't I carry a puppy?" cried Fluffy. "Please let me."

"You and Collie take turns!" ordered Lil' Red.

The group continued _ one block, two blocks, three blocks, four blocks, five blocks, six blocks. Red screamed, "Get down! Get down! Hit the bushes!"

They all observed a police car crossing the block in front of them. Laying with hearts beating ninety miles an hour and dry-mouthed, the group watched. Lil' Red whispered, "That was close! How much farther is it?"

Mark said, "Not too far. We can make it. We'll rest. That police car could take us back to the pound. If one of them comes again, run fast in all directions!"

Once more, the march began. This time Fluffy carried a puppy. There was a long path through a wooded area. "This will keep us off the road," Mark informed.

They kept their cautious move to the end of the overgrown park. Mark stopped. He held his tail straight and flipped it from side to side.

"What's wrong?" cried Lil' Red.

"Look at all those cars. I don't remember this. Oh, Red. I'm afraid I'm lost!" sighed Mark. Maybe we'll go back and I'll have to go see Peppie for directions.

"Oh no, this can't be far off. Think, doggone it! Think!" demanded Red.

Mark looked to the left, then to the right. He tried real hard to remember. Suddenly he began to sniff heavily in the air. He screamed, "Yes! Yes! It's this way! I remember that smell. It's over there. Look! The place is right over there on the comer."

"Oh Mark! Are you certain? That's a real big place; it's a castle. It's beautiful!" shook Lil' Red.

"Yes, Lil' Red. That's the place!" he replied. "We parked over there."

They heard the town clock pound seven bells.

"Look, come closer! Look, there are people on that porch. They are in a line in rocking chairs," Mark observed.

"Oh wow! I love riding in a rocking chair!" squealed Fluffy. "They go back and forth. Whoever drives it will hold you and rub you forever."

Lil' Red looked at each face carefully. Suddenly, she spotted a pretty grey-haired lady. Stepping closer, she knew it was Mumsie. "Oh my! Oh my! It's Mumsie! My Mumsie! Wait here for the signal."

Without any care Lil' Red began running across the street to get across to the comer that housed the beautiful retirement center. Horns from cars blew loudly and the squalling of the tires filled the air. All eyes followed the little red dachshund in fear. The folks on the porch stood crying and yelling.

Suddenly, Little Red seemed air-born and was motionless in the grass beside the sidewalk. The cars kept going and seemed to all disappear without concern. The people at the residence stared in disbelief

"Oh God, she's dead! She is killed," wept Fluffy.

A buzzing filled their ears. They could see the Praying Mantises flying to the beautiful lifeless dog. They got into position. The dogs began to cry. "Oh please let Lil' Red live! Please!"

As the prayer was complete, Lil' Red sat up shaking her head. The Mantis moved quickly to a nearby bush.

"It's a miracle! Look!" Fluffy gasped. "And look at Terry! His scar is gone. The rag worked too!"

Lil' Red waved then raced to the long porch. She saw Mumsie and began to cry. She raced to the woman and flew into her waiting arms.

Mumsie wept, "Oh Lil' Red, my precious baby! You found me. You almost died out there. I told you about cars. Oh little baby! I love you! I love you!"

All the humans watched the wonderful reunion. It was truly fantastic. Suddenly, Red stood and gave the *signal*. Her whole body shook as she raised her front paws.

The twenty animals took care crossing the road to join their friend.

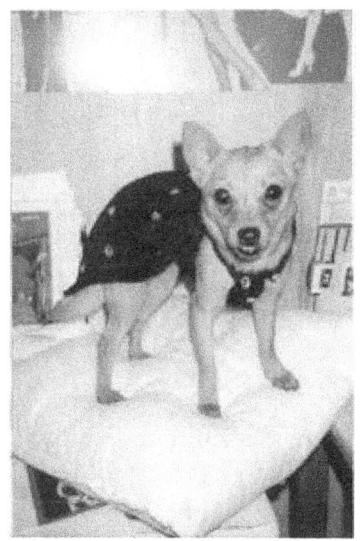

# Chapter 21

Lil' Red jumped back onto Mumsie's lap. She smiled happily watching the whole pack crossing the road. They stopped at the long brick walkway to place the baby animals with their mothers. Their procession was remarkable. Mark took the lead; Bonnie and her puppies came next; then Cat, Puss and kittens made the third group. They were already followed by the others – Terry, Fluffy, tiny Collie, Babe and big Bernie.

It was like a dream from Noah's Ark. They seemed to march two-by-two. The animals looked clean, beautiful, and inviting. One man stood and began to applaud, "Come on in, children! Come on in!"

Little Red rushed to accompany the group. She started toward Mumsie with Mark. Mumsie stood and started walking to them.

The old man grabbed a walker and shoved it in front of the woman. "Mumsie, here's your crutch; you're going to fall! Take your walker!"

"Horse feathers, I don't need that thing. I've got my baby back! Look, I can walk by myself!" Mumsie was amazed with herself. She was strutting like a teenager.

Lil' Red sat and held out a paw to the old man. He shook her hand laughing, "Little girl you're just like all women, conniving. You bat those big brown eyes and we melt. Who are your friends?"

Red fell to the floor and rolled for approval. Bonnie took her puppies around to the different people on the porch. She was followed by Puss, Cat, and kittens. The residents were so excited. They began to play and pet the little kittens.

Fluffy, Babe, Stray and Bernie stood by watching. They didn't want to push it. Mark laughed, "We're in! They love everybody. Look over there; the Praying Mantises are on that magnolia. Just take it easy. We still have our work cut out for us. "

The old man snickered, "I've about frozen to death every night. I'm taking this here Terrier and hiding him in my bed. Come on boy, I'll look after you, Terry-boy!"

Terry happily hid under his jacket. They left for his private room.

"I'm taking the cats and putting them in the chapel. It'll be nice for them. The preacher just comes on Sunday," smiled Roy, one of the attendants who looked after maintenance. "When I come back, I'd better do something with that huge dog. If Mrs. Berry sees them all at once she'll die!"

"No, we can't let anybody find out yet! We have to get a plan together. Everybody get you a baby and get to your room," commanded Geneva. "I'm taking this little baby collie. This is the cutest thing I've ever seen. She's a grown miniature collie. When I was a child, I had a big collie just like her."

"Be my dog!" Bernice whispered to Bonnie. "I can get your babies homes whenever they need one with my grandchildren. Come on, I live right at the end of the hall." She gathered all the puppies in her dress tail and told Bonnie to wait until she returned.

Fluffy felt dry-mouthed. She wanted somebody to want her. Abruptly, she shook all over and whined gently. Immediately, a woman looked at her. She put down her knitting and grinned happily, "Ain't that the cutest little thing you ever saw?"

"She can be yours Mozelle! Just pick her up and take her to your bed. You mustn't let anybody find her," smiled Johnny, a new resident. "I'm taking this greyhound. Now this is a beauty. I'll call her Babe. She's a real baby doll!"

"My poodle is so soft and fluffy. Look at her. I'll call her Fluff - no Fluffy!" explained Mozelle. "I always dreamed for a white dog."

Bernice returned for Bonnie.

Everyone had left the porch except Mark and Bernie. Mark said, "I can go to Lisa. Miss Rosie will take me there, but you need to get something. Too bad you're so huge."

"We'll talk to the Mantises. There's got to be a place for me. What about you? Can you really leave Lil' Red?" Bernie reminded Mark of his deep love and admiration for his friend.

"Gosh! Lisa would be taking me away from Red. No! I can't do that!" Mark growled and shot his ears up, "Let's go over there in the woods and think. Hurry before Roy gets back!"

"This crowd will have a better shot at things if I'm gone," cried Bernie. "I'm too big! I don't want to ruin things for the others."

"I'll get Peppie to take you to Lisa! She has a farm that's why she can have lots of dogs. Why didn't we think of that?" grinned Mark feeling relief. The two rushed across the street in the shadows. Things seemed to go smoothly. Mark and Bernie watched all the lights go off in the varied windows of the Sunnydale Retirement Center. For this night, all was well.

Inside the big residence, each animal was slipped into nice clean beds and cuddled close to human bodies. They were offered snacks and water. Each was told to use paper on the floor in the *bathroom*. They couldn't go outside until 6 :00 A.M.; even then, it had to be quick. Roy had agreed to take them out the windows while he pretended to be working in the yard.

Everything was cool for several weeks. In fact, the atmosphere at Sunnydale changed. People became different. The aides and nursing assistants entered into the *big secret*. Seeing the happiness the animals brought to each resident gave reason to keep the silence. It was complicated, the *big secret*, but worth it.

One morning an announcement blasted out on the intercom system: "All aides and assistants meet in the dining room at 10:00 sharp."

There was a big silence throughout the huge home; then, whispers. Never had an announcement as such been made.

Lil' Red cried, "Oh Praying Mantises, please help us!"

Mumsie burst out in tears, "I'll never let you go! Never! They can kill me! We'll always be together. Just wait! I'll call Rosie and her kid. They'll fix anything that needs fixing!"

Mozelle slipped Fluffy into the large closet, "Stay put honey, and it'll be alright!"

Bernice grumbled, "Bonnie take your babies under the bed and feed them. Hide! It's going to be alright."

Johnny rushed Babe into her little bedroom he had created in a comer.

The old man kissed Terry's nose and placed him amongst the bed pillows. "Sh-sh-sh! Play like you're a stuffed animal."

Roy took the felines to the greenhouse where they played daily.

Geneva stuck her head out the door and bolted, "They can have all my B.C. powders, but Collie stays. She's my best medicine. I think we're in trouble."

It became 10:00 very quickly. Everybody that had to go to this irregular meeting showed up pronto. Each filed into the big room with sadness.

Roy whispered, "At least they can't fire us all! It's too hard to replace us!"

Their faces looked grey and lifeless as they dropped into their seats. When coffee, juice and cookies were offered, nobody responded. It wasn't a time to celebrate. Finally, the twelve helpers who had been summoned were awaiting their deepest fear – *caught hiding animals with the residents*. They'd hear about hair in the carpet, dandruff air, and probably smells they imagined. They nervously waited.

Ms. Susan, the CEO and director, rushed to the head table. Her expensive cobalt suit clung to her tall, delicate figure. She was very beautiful and sophisticated. Mostly, she was real good to the residents and fair with the employees. Now, everyone felt a line had been crossed.

The double doors had been closed. With a huge bang, one flew open. Rosie rushed in and sat down. Becky and Lisa followed. This bewildered the staff. They too were dressed in the somber sexy suits that clung like silk. One wore plum and the other a velvety green.

Outside, all residents waited. Geneva had a large glass. She placed it against the wall and laid her ear on it. She slipped her finger to her lips urging quiet. "Listen," she whispered.

You could hear a pin drop. In the distance, a cow gave a big moo. Bonnie, being a beagle, had to answer, "Ohhhh-owh-ohhh!"

Nobody wanted to hear that. Perspiration broke out on their faces; their hands turned clammy. Caught for sure.

Their ears rang with the spoon tinkling against a glass.

Ms. Susan began, "We have something going on here that is very unique. In the last month, there have been changes – unusual changes. We've got to get to the bottom of it!"

The employees continued to sweat and felt near heart attacks coming on. Under his breath Roy muttered, "Maybe it was illegal – we're going to jail!"

Ms. Susan continued, "I'm so amazed. First, Mumsie stops using a walker and began to smile. She is happy. Mozelle is no long having migraines. Bernice is knitting more and teaching a class making strange tiny sweaters. Johnny is wearing his teeth and eating. 'Ole Man' is talking and joking. And, Roy, why are you so involved with the greenhouse and chapel?"

Everybody looked at each other in shock and fear.

Ms. Susan smiled, "What is the change? Our people are happy. Some are gaining weight; some have given up pills that covered loneliness and pain. My reports show a complete turnaround for all of our residents. If we aren't careful, they'll be gone!"

Roy stood, "Ms. Susan, it's about their prayers being answered. They had been praying for love."

Ms. Susan replied, "Love is life extending and helps to bridge sadness. Everybody needs love. It all changed after Rosie and her girls had their show here. What kind of spell did you case, Rosie?"

Rosie smiled, "No spell, I don't know!"

Ms. Susan asked, "Your friend Mumsie has thrown away pills, walker and looks so good. She smiles all the time! What is it?"

Roy rushed out the door, "I'll be right back!"

Ms. Susan kept trying to find out what had happened. It was very apparent that life was better at Sunnydale Retirement Center, but the secret wasn't out yet.

After a very short time, Roy opened the double doors and yelled, "Tah-da-da! Here's your answer Ms. Susan!"

Mumsie was first inside with Lil' Red strutting beside her on a leash. They smiled happily, "I have my baby now Ms. Susan. She is everything I need. She makes me happy. I never knew how important Lil' Red was. I'm sorry 1 hid her, but I have to keep her now."

Next, Johnny strolls in with Babe; Bernice carried the puppies in a flower basket she found in the trash and mother dog Bonnie followed. Geneva coaxed miniature collie through the door with a piece of chocolate. Old Man urged Terry to join the others. Roy stepped outside and motioned to Cat, Puss and the kittens. "Come on! We need you!"

The workers were amazed seeing them all together and exclaimed "Oh-h-h-h?"

Mozelle sachets to the front of the room and stood eye to eye with Mrs. Berry. Tears rolled down her cheek as she placed her beautiful white poodle on the table. The dog sat and started to quiver.

Ms. Susan touched her soft head with her professionally manicured fingers. She smiled, "You are darling!"

Mozelle snapped, "Go on, take her! I ain't got nothing else left. They took my house, most of my clothes, my car, my jewels and the garden. Ain't nothing left but to die! Be good to my Fluffy, Ms. Susan!"

Everyone broke into a screaming and crying jag. They fell onto each other's shoulders boo-hooing. The animals cried with them. It was a historic sad moment; one never to be forgotten.

Roy sternly projected, "This is so pitiful. All everyone needs is love. Look at the difference this last month made. Even those without personal pets found love and emotional nutrition."

Rosie, Becky and Lisa had left the room but were returning. Shock filled the room of people. Peppie, Zipper, Spike, Mark and Bernie marched in.

"Oh my God!" whispered Ms. Susan and fainted. Someone blocked her fall to the floor and was licking her face when she became conscious; it was Bernie. She got to her feet with assistance to add, "Where were we? I mean just what can we do?"

Lisa said, "Keep them all – they make a real difference in the heart. You can see that already. Now the last group that came in is ours."

Becky grabbed tiny Zipper and scratched his chest. "Zipper's a sweet boy! He's wonderful – a little old, but perfect. Keep these babies here. Can't you understand how a pet just fills that void in a person's life?"

Rosie added, "That's right! If I'm talking to myself and Peppie is around, people think I'm speaking to her. When by yourself, they insist you're crazy."

"Say no more, this is a dilemma!" scribed Ms. Susan. "I could just hold anyone of these beautiful creatures and eat 'em with love!"

Everyone looked at each other. All employees and all residents were hanging onto every word and motion.

"Lisa, how can we do this?" Ms. Susan asked.

"Real easy!" she smiled.

Becky plotted, "We can have an inside wire fence for them to separate the 'potty area' from the other. Roy can find someone to maintain that."

"Sure! Sure!" he exclaimed. "Anything you say! The kitties love the greenhouse! I can fix their place there all seven of them. They've already gotten rid of the mice out there."

A cook held her hand up.

"Yes, Arlene?" recognized the CEO.

"I needs to borrows some of those cats fo' my kitchen. *Mices* runs around at night sometimes," she explained. "I won't keep them all the time now. Maybe that fat white cat can do the job."

It was now an accepted fact all the new animal residents were home. The flight from the pound had paid off for them.

Lisa swooped down to cuddle with the huge Saint Bernard. "Bernie, I would love to have you go back to my farm with me. I work for a veterinarian and we can support a monster like this."

Rosie was surprised. "Oh Lisa, he needs a home too! That's wonderful. What about this dog that 'wets' on the trees and bushes?"

"He can be mine!" pleaded Ms. Susan. "I'll call him Mark. He is marked so beautifully!"

"Oh no! I just made a phone call. Dr. Bob will be here with a mobile clinic in an hour. Every one of our pets will be completely checked. They'll be tested for diseases, fungus, mites, lice, worms and all other physical enemies. He will maintain a health card for each one. "

"Even the kitties and puppies?" Bernice quizzed.

"All creatures!" Becky added.

"Right! But the kicker is everyone get spayed or neutered if they haven't been!" ruled Lisa.

Cats' eyes rolled and he jumped on top a table screaming in cat language, "Oh no! You're gonna do that to me?"

Bernie grunted, "All of us, they've been listening to Bob Barker on TV say, 'Have your pet neutered or spayed to control the pet population!"

"Well I'm glad!" smiled Bonnie.

"Me too!" laughed Puss flipping her long tail watching her litter of kittens rolling on the floor. "Look at them. So cute, even so, I couldn't take that again!"

Lil' Red grinned, "A small price to pay for a wonderful home." She cuddled next to Mumsie. Looking out the big picture window, she pointed.

The animals smiled. They could see the Praying Mantises hanging on a bush beside the wall. They each settled quickly into their prayer position. "Thank you for home.

THE END

# Part II
# Treats Recipes for Candies

## POOCH BISCOTTI
*(For medium to large dogs)*

- 1 baked chicken (separate meat from heavy bones)
- 2 1/2 c. shredded (breast gristle, fat and skin)
- 2 Tbsp. finely chopped parsley, (fresh is best)
- 3/4 c. shredded cheddar cheese
- 1 Tbsp. garlic, minced
- 1 (14 ½ oz.) can drained green beans
- 2/3 c. oats (oatmeal) beaten fme
- 1 (1/4 oz.) pkg. Yeast
- 1 c. cornmeal
- 2 c. whole wheat flour
- 2 Tbsp. bone meal
- 1 tsp. salt
- ¼ tsp. grits
- 2 eggs, beaten
- ¼ c. evaporated milk
- ¼ c. molasses or Karo syrup
- ½ stick margarine or butter or canola oil
- 1 extra egg

Chop together the chicken, bones, fat and skin. Add parsley, cheddar cheese, garlic and green beans; chop together. In separate bowl mix together oats, yeast, cornmeal, flour, bone meal, salt and grits. To flour mixture, add 2 eggs, evaporated milk, molasses and margarine; mix well. Add chopped mixture to flour mixture; blend well. Turn out onto wheat-floured table;

knead a few minutes to bring together in a ball. Let rest for ½ hour or so.

Roll out to ½" thick; cut with biscuit cutter or shaped cookie cutters. Beat 1 egg and brush over biscuits. Bake at 350°F about 35 minutes or until light brown. Leave in turned off oven for harder biscotti. May freeze to keep long-term.

Make smaller biscuits for smaller pets.

*Chicken can be substituted with turkey or ground beef.

## POOCHIE PRALINES

- 1 cup Corn Flakes
- 1 cup Rice Krispies
- 1 cup peanut butter
- 1 egg
- ½ cup milk
- ¼ cup bone meal
- ½ tsp. salt
- 2 Tbsp. corn syrup

- Mix all ingredients well. Place on cookie sheet in tablespoons. Bake in 350° oven for about 20 to 30 minutes. Enjoy! Can freeze.

## MEATY LOAF

- 1 cup ground hamburger
- 1 cup cooked rice
- 1 Tbsp. garlic powder
- 1 tsp. salt (sprinkle over)
- ½ c. shredded cheddar cheese
- 1 egg
- ½ cup water
- Mix together well. Use oven dish about 4" x 9" x 4". (Spray dish with oil). Place mixture evenly in dish.
- Bake about 25 minutes or until brown at 375°. (A toaster oven works well).

NOTE: Animals don't like food real hot. I have a small dog about 10 lbs. She gets this in four servings as a special meal. Of course, she has her regular dry food available. Keep extra portions in refrigerator several days or freeze for later use.

## DOGGIE PATTIES

- (Cheeseburgers)
- 1/2 cup ground turkey
- 1/2 cup ground beef
- 6 cooked and chopped slices of bacon
- 1 Tbsp. garlic (chopped)

- 1 tsp. onion powder
- 1/2 tsp. salt
- 1 cup cooked rice
- 1/2 cup sour cream
- 2 eggs (raw)

Mix all together well. Roll into patties. (Freeze uncooked if desired). Cook in frying pan or grill – even the George Foreman grill is great. Cook to medium (not well). Serve them cut up. *Don't let the children steal them!*

## TURKEY LOAF

- (Use turkey leftovers or bake a small turkey portion). Cook turkey in foil about 30 minutes per pound until done.
- Remove any bones. Cut off the part you may want for yourself and set aside. Chop or grind the balance of the meat.
- 2 cups cooked, prepared Turkey (with gristle okay)
- 1/2 cup oatmeal
- 1 cup rice (cooked or use minute uncooked)
- 1 Tbsp. chopped garlic or fresh
- 1/2 tsp. salt
- 1 finely chopped small onion
- 1/2 cup broth from turkey (or canned turkey broth)
- 1/2 tsp. yellow cake color (optional)
- 1/2 cup finely chopped nuts
- 2 eggs (raw)

- Mix together well. Spray Pam in 8" x 8" x 2" baking dish and pour in mixture; even with spoon. Bake in 375° oven about 35 minutes. Cut into servings. Store by freezing.

## PUP POPS

- (Good for humans!)
- A wonderful treat for your "*baby*" and so simple to make. My dog "Peppie" wants to share my ice cream. I don't like giving her this. I'm not certain "people" ice cream is good for an animal. Thus, she's very happy with her "pup pop" Let me share this with you.
- Ingredients for **Peanut Butter Pop**:
- 1 cup peanut butter
- 1 cup sour cream
- 1 cup water
- 4 drops yellow cake color
- 71/2 teaspoon vanilla flavoring
- 1/4 cup 7oatmeal or five crushed English walnuts 7
- Mix well a7nd pour into ice trays; place in freezer. After7 frozen well, remove from ice trays and place in plastic freezer bag. Return to freezer and give to pet as desired. *Remember! Stay outta them yourself!*

NOTE: You can place Popsicle stick in each when 1/2 frozen.

*Use same directions for the following Pup Pop recipes. Enjoy!

### INGREDIENTS FOR COCONUT-WALNUT POP:

- 1/2 cup coconut
- 1/2 cup coconut milk
- 1 cup sour cream
- Small packet of Equal
- 1 cup finely chopped English walnuts
- 1/2 cup oatmeal
- Ingredients for **Cherry-Nut Pop**:
- 1 cup crushed Maraschino cherries and its juice
- 1 cup sour cream
- 1/2 cup yogurt (plain or cherry flavor)
- 1/2 cup oatmeal
- 1/2 cup crushed peanuts
- 1/2 cup water
- 1 pkg. Sweet 'n Low
- (A larger recipe because of more liquid).
- Ingredients for **Honey Cream Pop**:
- 1/2 cup honey
- 1 cup sour cream
- 1/2 cup plain yogurt
- 1 pkg. Sweet 'n Low
- 1/2 cup oatmeal
- 1/2 cup crushed peanuts

## DOGGIE DIPS

- 1 cup self-rising coarse corn meal
- 1/2 cup plain flour
- 1/2 cup oatmeal
- 1/2 cup bone meal (purchase from health food store)
- 1 egg
- 1 cup sour cream
- 1/2 cup oil (bacon drippings or ham are okay!)
- 1 tsp. salt
- 1 pkg. sweetener (Sweet 'n Low)
- Mix well. For larger dogs double recipe and make a size larger.

SPLIT INTO 3 PARTS. PLACE IN SMALL MIXING BOWLS. TO ONE PART ADD:

- 1 small squash chopped
- 1/2 small onion
- 1 tsp. garlic
- 1/4 cup canned corn
- Keep hands floured. Mix in and roll out into penny-size balls. Place on cookie sheet. Cook in pre-heated oven at 350° for about 45 minutes. They should be crispy but not real hard. Dump immediately onto towel. Cool and place in plastic bags.
- Using another 1/3 part, add:
- 1 10.5 oz. can Banner sausage

- 1 cup oatmeal
- 1 egg
- 1 tsp. garlic
- Mix well. Roll with well-floured hands onto floured surface. Make into a long roll about a foot-long shape square. Cut in half and then slice ¼" thick. Place into a 350° oven for about 45 minutes or until crispy done. (These make take a bit longer). When done slide onto towel to completely cool before placing into storage bags. (For long keeping, freeze).
- To the third part add:
- 1 large can tuna fish
- 1 small can green beans or carrots
- 1 large egg
- Mix gently by throwing with a fork. Take tablespoons of the mixture with floured hands and roll in disc, then flatten to 1/4". Cook in 350° oven for about 40 to 50 minutes (not too crispy). When done, place "Dippers" on paper towel. Cool before serving or freezing. (Cats like this too!).

## PEANUT BUTTER TREAT

- 1 cup crunchy peanut butter
- 1/2 stick butter
- 2 Tbsp. Karo syrup
- 1 cup flour
- 1 egg
- 1 Tbsp. cinnamon
- Mix well. Place onto cookie sheet by large tablespoons. Bake in 325° oven until light brown (about 20-28 minutes).

## CHICKEN TRAINING STRIPS

- 4 (halves) chicken breast
- 3 Tbsp. olive oil – salt to taste, lemon-pepper
- 1 cup crushed Waverly crackers
- 1 cup 2% milk
- 1/2 cup crushed pecans or walnuts
- Cut breast halves in 6 long strips. Wash and dry. Salt to taste. Dip each piece of chicken into milk (placed in a shallow bowl). Place in a 2" x 8" x 10" baking dish lined with olive oil. Sprinkle nuts, lemon-pepper over. Cover with foil. Bake in 365° oven about 20 to 30 minutes. Makes great training strips. For now or freeze for later.

## RICE TREATS

- 1 cup rice (washed)
- ½ tsp. salt
- Place in 2 cups hot water. Bring to boil; then simmer (lowest) about 20 minutes (stir occasionally). If too dry, add a little water.
- **Split into 3 parts** (Make 3 different flavors)
- 1 part cooked rice
- 1/2 lb. Ground beef (salt to taste)
- 1 Tbsp. garlic
- 1 cup chopped peanuts
- 3 Tbsp. water
- 1 Tbsp. corn starch

Pan fry beef; add salt, garlic and peanuts. Pour off all oil. Add rice and stir. Mix cornstarch with water and pour over; stir. Roll into balls and place in oven pan. Bake 10 minutes at 350°.

### A. 1 part cooked rice
- 1 small can of peas
- 8 oz. shredded cheese
- Mix lightly. Make into balls. Bake 10 minutes at 350°. Serve or keep.

### B. 1 part cooked rice
- 1/2 pkg. wieners (chopped well)
- 3 Tbsp. mayonnaise
- 4 oz. American cheese (shredded)

- 1/4 cup sour cream
- Mix and make into balls. Bat 10 minutes at 350°. Cool. Serve or keep.

## DOGGIE CRACKER DIP

- 1/2 cup sour cream
- 1/4 cup can milk
- 1/2 cup melted Velveeta cheese
- 1/2 cup parsley (for good breath)
- 1/4 tsp. salt
- 1/4 tsp. garlic (rid fleas)
- Mix together. Place over or with crackers or Doggie Dip. (As an appetizer).

## *GOOD MANNERS FOR DOGS*

1. Eating at a breakfast bar is a treat for many pets. It gives a sense of security. Usually, they eat well with company.

2. Stem-wear in plastic or glass is a nice touch. Dog can drink without bending down so far. *Nice china is always wonderful!

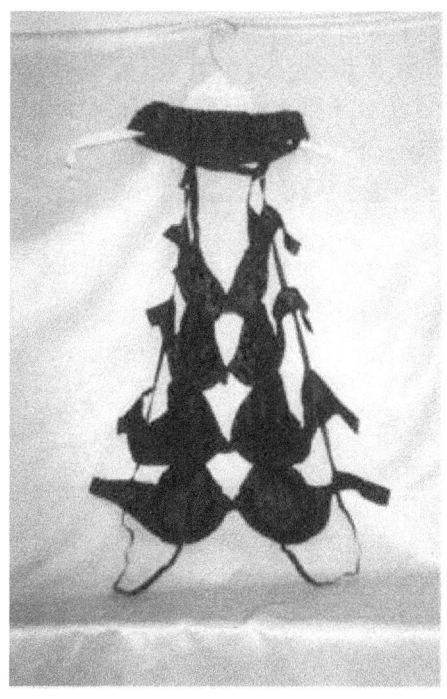

# CANDY

(A Short Story)

Dogs were barking from every house in the neighborhood. One suddenly squealed over all of the others, crying with some kind of trauma. The moon was huge, in fact totally full. It was almost as if it were after dusk rather than midnight. When Sarah Benson stopped her car in the drive at her back door, the big white Husky usually came happily from her square house tucked next to the edge of the big house. The chain hooked to the clothesline allowed the animal to move freely over the side yard.

Sarah opened her door so "Candy" could greet her in the usual manner. She snapped the chain from the collar and hurried to open the house. Instantly, the creature slipped past to 'the bowls on the floor of the kitchen. She lapped water.

"Patient! Girl! I know my baby is hungry! I'll get it for you!" she spoke aloud to the dog. "I'll pour your milk first! I've got a new canned food! It's Senior Alpo! *Zipper* used to love this!"

The dog lay beside the bowls waiting as if she understood every word. Immediately, the milk came, then the Alpo.

"You'd better eat that! I'll give it to that black pussycat!" teased Sarah. "I missed you today! I brought you a real bone! Look! T-bone! After you eat, you can take it out on the deck!"

Sarah had warmed green beans and corn in the microwave for herself. Candy stared at each bite from table to mouth.

"Alright! I'll share even if you didn't," laughed Sarah. She scooped a good part into the dog bowl and of course the dog consumed it and wanted more. "Here, take this bone! You need your teeth cleaned anyhow!"

The beast greedily took the bone to her house rug and began tearing it, chewing and pulling.

Their continual five years of such routine was the way of life with Sarah and "Candy" Benson. The dog was the perfect pet, attractive, affectionate and quite devoted.

When it was time for Candy to be sent to the fenced back yard for the night, the neighborhood dogs were once more ranting their anger at whatever was disturbing them.

"Maybe a deer ran through!" guessed Sarah.

Candy flapped her tail as if in agreement. She cocked her head and brought her ears to a full point; there was loud movement. The dog rushed in the direction with an excited whine.

"Easy!" whispered Sarah, "Easy girl! It's the deer! Wow! One! Two! Three! Four! Oh my gosh! There's over a dozen! Easy girl!"

The dog sat down and watched. The deer didn't seem to even notice and kept picking leaves from the bushes.

"I knew rabbits weren't eating that many apples! Oh well! Leave them alone and go to bed!" ordered Sarah.

Candy had sat quiet as long as she could stand it. She just had to prove she was boss. Rushing toward the fence, she gave a low growling bark. The nearest deer stood on his back feet then jumped nearly straight up. It was over, they alerted each other and took off deeper into the big trees and brush.

Panting with a wide smile, Candy hurried to sit beside Sarah.

"It's alright! The idiots would get the garden anyhow!" smiled Sarah and patted Candy. Once more, the dogs around began barking.

With cupped hands Sarah screamed, "Shut up!" Immediately, everything was totally quiet from bark and the locust filled the air with their strange noise.

Routine with Candy was very pleasant. A dog like Candy was absolute company and there was always that special camaraderie. It felt good to come home knowing she was there. Candy loved walks and jogging. She would rush after a frisbee as long as someone would play. She would get peculiar with any visitors she thought were not friends, always listening for the command from Sarah.

Living alone was a choice Sarah selected. She liked privacy. Her work in the home-office required involved concentration. Candy didn't interfere with this.

The adage, "Man's best friend is his dog!" probably is one of the greatest truths. If an animal is treated with a little love and kindness, he'll follow you to the end. With love the pet gets better and better. Candy and Sarah were that kind of companions.

Many dogs hate gunshot, storms and blasting sounds. Actually, some noises hurt their ears. Sometimes strangers tease animals when they catch the owner away. Candy was one in the category of not liking fireworks and blasts. Even so, her duty to guard was prevalent.

Anyone who has ever loved a pet would cherish the existence of Candy. Once, a neighbor kid coaxed her to go home with him. Even though he tied her at home,

Candy managed to get loose and found her way home. The pet was about four years old when Sarah acquired her. A business changed hands and Sarah took her in. Over the years the gratitude and love thickened.

Then, one humid summer night, Sarah drove in their yard. Candy didn't greet her. It was real late. By the time the door was unlocked and Candy had not come; Sarah felt a pit-in-the-stomach ache.

"Candy!" she called softly then looked into the empty doghouse. "Candy! Where's my girl?"

From a short distance away, there was a weak cry. Sarah found the dog trying to come to her. She sat with her front feet trying to pull her backside along. Candy was in pain; with each movement she cried out.

Knowing a hurt dog can bite, Sarah was careful with her greeting and tried to discover what was wrong. At first glance she saw two bloody places in the middle of the back. This was the spot to avoid.

A neighbor swung the corner in his pickup. Sarah jumped and rushed toward him, "Help me!"

He stopped fast, "Sarah! What's wrong? Are you alright?"

She broke into tears, "No! It's Candy! She's hurt! Please help me!"

No more had to be said. The two retraced Sarah's steps back toward the whimpering dog. Sarah stopped to pick up a rug from Candy's house.

"She's here!"

"Oh wow! She is hurt!"

"Oh, Candy, my poor girl. I'm so sorry you're hurt. Lean against me and let me hold you!" cried Sarah as she encircled the white Husky in her arms. As she rocked the dog gently, the animal seemed to calm and responded somewhat.

"This is terrible! Wonder what happened?" the neighbor prodded. "She never bothered anyone! Sometimes she'd bark!"

"I know!" sniffed Sarah. "Can you stay with her? Let me go in the house a minute. I'll be right back!"

"Sure! Take your time!" he assured.

Nearly feeling panicky, Sarah raced through the door and straight to the medicine cabinet. As she snapped open a bottle the pills flew out onto the counter. She forced her tears back and said aloud, "Alright! Take it easy! Get her a Tylenol – yes, cut one of these muscle relaxes in half, that will help her! This surgical salve and a razor, get it! A couple towels, yeah! All right! A light, a flashlight! Gloves! Yes! Rubber gloves!"

With her emergency items, she returned.

"Help me ease her on this rug! Careful! Take her backside; she might bite!" cautioned the woman. "I'll be able to look at her better now."

Flashing the light across the hurt canine, Sarah could already see the blood-splotched spots. The thick fur disguised the situation and at first look it seemed like just a bit of bleeding.

Sarah held the dog close with an arm firmly around her neck forcing the head tight to her shoulder. The close investigation took place under the flashlight beam held by the neighbor. With her gloved hands, Sarah carefully moved her fingers gently down the dog's back. She gave a painful moan but allowed the checkup.

"She's been shot! I'll bet a thousand dollars! Some sorry crumb has shot her!" moaned Sarah. "Let's go on and get her to the deck! Let me unsnap this chain!"

Using the little rug as a stretcher, the two moved the dog carefully to the porch. They settled her there. Stroking the baby, Sarah directed the man to retrieve the supplies she'd left on the ground.

In his absence, she picked the pills from her pocket, licked them and threw them to the back of the dog's throat. She wrapped her hand around the now closed mouth and rubbed her throat. "This will help you baby! I'm so sorry!

Waiting just a few minutes, the dog relaxed more and her breathing seemed to slow to a more normal pace. Sarah started clearing an area on each side of her spine with a finger then the razor. Finally, the surgical salve was smeared over the two holes on each side of the spine. The dog was paralyzed and unable to walk. The medication quickly put the dog to sleep. She was at least out of misery for the moment.

"Come in!" offered Sarah, then opened the door. "Can you believe this?"

"It's crazy! Just crazy! I saw her about 9:00 when I left for town. She was all right then! Maybe she just hurt herself!"

"We'll see! It's too late to do anymore tonight. I know somebody shot her!"

"Wouldn't it kill her?" he questioned sipping the coffee put before him.

"Maybe, she may not make it through the night. All I know to do now is hope she can recover. The medicine will keep her quiet. It's up to God!" whispered Sarah turning away to cry.

It was a long night. Sarah was up and down checking on Candy. She repeated the medicines about 6:00 A.M.; once more the dog lay to rest. Again, about 10:00, it was medication time. She brought the dog into the house carefully.

"Baby, maybe you can eat something!" smiled Sarah. "How about a scrambled egg with cheese bacon and some milk coffee? I know you love that!"

Once breakfast was done, she placed it neatly on a bed tray. Quickly, she clipped a rose and stuck it into a bud vase. She sat it on the floor beside Candy. As Sarah ate her portion, she offered the pet a bite but the dog refused anything. Her nose was hot and dry too. At least the comfort of air conditioning would help as well as being away from any outside environment.

When Sarah talked with the vet, he said to bring her in the next day if she didn't respond. Maybe it was a dog bite and she would come around.

Things stayed the same until the next day. Finally at noon, Candy ate a handful of dog food and a cup of water. This was somewhat hopeful. That afternoon, Candy was placed in the veterinarian's care. They would x-ray and go over her status. Sarah was to call the next day.

Finally, the next day came around and nervously Sarah made the phone call.

"How is Candy?" she asked when the doctor was on the other end of the line.

"No change! We x-rayed, you were right. She was shot!"

"Oh, no!"

"It was a shotgun, two times! I counted almost thirty or so pellets still in her. It's not good! There's tremendous nerve damage and she's still paralyzed."

"Can she recover?"

"Very doubtful, but we can wait and see!"

The next week seemed slow moving. Having made several visits to see Candy, Sarah began to realize the bleakness of the situation. She lost sleep and missed the old faithful friend. On the last visit, she held the dog close and exchanged all the love she could find.

The doctor had showed her the x-rays and explained this kind of nerve damage could not be repaired in any way. The dog could only lay with the mercy of those around her. She might drag her paralyzed backside behind. She could not care for her hygiene needs; control was gone.

Finally, with a heavy heart, and tears Sarah bid the once beautiful animal goodbye. The time had come to let go and release the dog from further suffering. Her hands trembled as she closed the lower cage. Candy looked sad and blinked her brown eyes.

The doctor stood by the door waiting and knowing.

"There's nothing that will help?"

"No, it's unfortunate. I had to have my dog put down last year for cancer. This is a tough thing to do!" he consoled.

"I guess it has to be!" Sarah broke down.

An assistant walked in and mumbled, "I'm truly sorry!"

The doctor patted Sarah on the shoulder; "We'll take it from here. Are you all right? Will you be able to drive?"

"Yes! I knew it was coming; it's just so much harder than I thought! All my other dogs have died of old age!" sniffed Sarah. "Let me pay."

"Come with me!" smiled the young girl with the clinic. She placed Sarah in a comfortable inner office.

Once everything was finalized, Sarah walked through the full waiting room with people and their pets. Her eyes were red and filled with tears. Sympathy spilled over from the people around who could empathize. Many whispered they were sorry and several asked if they could help.

One woman and her daughter knew Sarah, "Do you need me to drive for you? We know how much it hurts!"

"But this is different; Candy was murdered! Shot for no reason!" uttered Sarah.

"Well, what goes around comes around!" deemed a man sitting with two terriers in a basket. "I'd kill the person."

"It wouldn't do any good. Whoever did it will always know they did it. One day, something will bring it back," insisted the woman who came to Sarah's aid. "You have to let it go!"

"I know! Nothing will ever change it. I've had some great years with Candy. I'll enjoy those memories forever," Sarah tried to adjust.

There was a small museum near the vet's clinic. Sarah browsed there for about an hour. She collected her emotions to return home. The emptiness met the grieving woman when she entered the driveway.

The word spread through the neighborhood about Candy. Neighbors were shocked and contributed their condolences. Soon it was discovered Candy was number four dog in the cul-de-sac to die under suspicious conditions.

The third day after Candy's passing, Sarah was watering her roses when she heard a clamor of high-pitched voices. Feeling down, Sarah ignored the commotion until it stopped beside her. Looking up, she saw four of the neighbor children. They had their hands full of wildflowers and six dogs on leashes with another group of dogs following.

It was as if they all had been instructed to be reverent. The children stood with somber faces, while the dogs each sat looking at Sarah.

One little girl about eight years old spoke up, "We're so sorry about Candy! We brought you these flowers!"

Touched, Sarah smiled, "Thanks you so much! That is so nice of you."

They handed their bouquets to the woman with happy smiles.

"Well, Ms. Benson, we'll miss Candy too. But we decided to bring all these "extra dogs" for you to pick out the one you want. Maybe it can take Candy's place. Now that one, the brown mixed-up one there, that belongs to Mrs. Gray. She's not nice to him anyhow; he could use a better home. Mrs. Gray is real hateful!"

Sarah laughed, "How nice of all of you! I do appreciate this! Maybe I'd better wait to get another dog! Would you like some cake, milk, coffee or tea?"

"Wow that would be great!" gleed a little boy with beads of perspiration on his nose. "I ain't ever had coffee!"

"Come on in!" smiled Sarah. "You can help me plan a memorial for Candy. I'll get her ashes on Friday."

"Oh great! A real dog funeral!" screamed one.

"Yes, and we'll have a dog show too with all your dogs," planned Sarah.

"That's neat!" smiled a six-year-old as he entered with his Dalmatian on a leash.

After all the children and animals had entered the kitchen, Sarah served everyone a nice hunk of cake she had frosted earlier. They talked all at one time with their plans to "remember" Candy.

"My dog was shot too!" cried a little girl. "We found her beside the road."

"We'll have the funeral for all of the deceased dogs," offered Sarah.

"De-ceased?" asked a child not understanding the word.
"Yes!" another cut in. "It means she "de-sees," like you don't sees her ever again!"

THE END

Remembering "Casy" Hunt
12 years old - Died November, 2005
Who Am I?
Here I sit in my yard
It's fenced; I can't go far –
But I can think like a dog,
Of pleasant times in a fog.
I see the spots on my coat
Black on white softly boast.
I can hide here in the rocks
Watching birds perch in flocks.
If I stay here long enough –
I'll be a diamond in the rough.
A "Rock-wilder" thought I could be –
Glaring for passersby to see.
I growl at times a forbidden sound,
To see outsiders run and frown.
Well, I guess I settle now to be –
The Dalmatian, I guess you see!
Rotha J. Dawkins

Rotha J. Dawkins

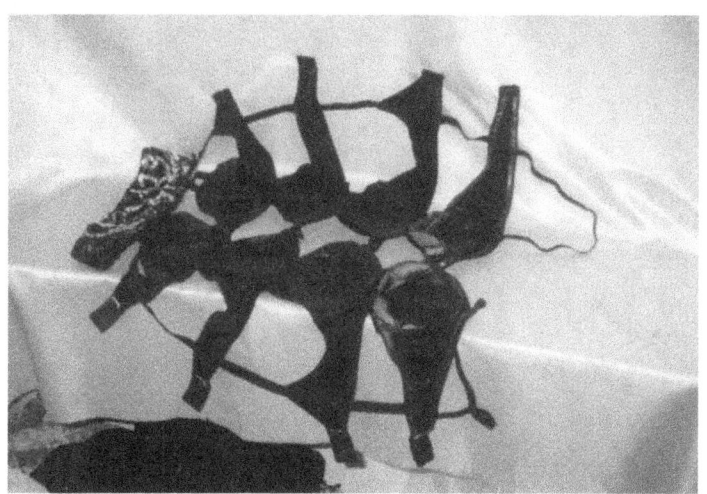

# Part III
# Treats
# Dressing Your Dog

## DOG BRA

Strange? It is different but some pets need a little help. Often a dog that is breast-feeding needs something. At times, her breasts may be sore from the puppies' toenails or a scratch from another source. The mothers' breasts often feel so heavy that support helps. Large busted dogs have often had several litters.

You can make this for your pet. Most of the breasts that will need help will be eight. They, of course, will be side by side in twos. Just roll the animal over and count and look for the placement. Sketch on a piece of paper the layout of your dogs' stomach. Give the measurements of the placement for each tit. Start at the bottom inside her back legs and layout to the top tits.

Things you will need:
1. Four small sized bras (readymade) probably size 28A or 32A or such. Check with your thrift stores for these and have them close in style and color. Making this custom fit and style gives you lots of room for design and creativity.
2. Needles, thread and routine sewing equipment are needed.
3. Have available extra 1/2 inch and 3/4 inch elastic.
4. A 12-inch piece of fun fabric. It can be satin, velvet, or any plain or fancy material. It will be for the collar.

5. Remove the straps from all bras. (Shoulder straps)
6. Keep all straps for later use.
7. Place all four bras front-side down on your pattern layout.
8. Pin each bra, bottoms to top in the area where the original straps had been on front/cup area. Bras will be in a row. Sew into place.

For "back" straps. (Cut off at back leaving about 4" of strap.) Sew each bra for connection adjusted to your pet.

# "WEARINGS"

Introducing your pet to wearing clothes can be interesting. My son had a very strong and temperamental large Dalmatian. Not just anyone could touch her. Years ago, I was her pal. She had never forgotten. With age, she became calmer; then developed a bit of arthritis. I made her two sweaters I thought would give her comfort.

She was in and outdoors as she pleased so color and fabric was to be considered. I selected a fairly tight knit with red, white and blue stripes; very good for her breed. With her white with black spots, all colors worked. Dalmatians shed so the loose hair is there. A great plus for sweaters; they will collect a great deal of the shedding fur.

My grand-dog Casey would smile showing all of her teeth. I let her sniff and check out the sweaters, then explained to her how nice the garments were and how they would feel good. Quickly, I showed her a dog treat. Bribing, she let me put on the beautiful striped outfit. She understood and made the first trade to slip the item over her head. With two more treats each front leg was put through their hole designated for comfort.

With another real special treat (a small "greenie"), I praised Casey telling her how beautiful she looked and how nice the sweater was. My son, William, was quite surprised. The children were totally excited. Casey enjoyed the attention. Soon, she went outside to sleep and dropped onto a warm place against the house in her garment. She wore the sweater for the rest of the day.

My daughter, Rebekah, has a tiny Dachshund. He's a slick little black fellow with age (about 11 years). That takes its toll on his thinning coat that is already very short. "Zipper" shivers and wraps into blankets. He was my first animal to need sweaters. Small short-hair dogs often need protection from the cold weather. Most pets will wear clothes best if there are no sleeves in the tops. Of course, it takes a bit of training for the bottom side (or hips and tail).

People love their pets ("babies") and love having extras for them. Always keep in mind these particulars:
   a. Safety - <u>Garments should be worn when being attended. They should be able to fully get out of the garment. Make them so they cannot hang themselves or eat items that could choke them.</u>
   b. Washable - This is best for continual use.
   c. Colors - I still believe animals see more than black and white. Who really knows? (Maybe some vet is a reincarnated dog!)
   d. Garments supply a barrier between a drafty floor and the pet.
   e. Closures:
1. Snaps – fixed tightly.
2. Buttons – want to chew them – must be where pet cannot get to them.
3. Velcro – good. But, when washing, be certain to "close" garment. Velcro will attach to every string in the washer and has the ability to tear at garments.

4. *Tie ups* – be very cautious; a pet could hang itself.
5. *Elastic* – great! Can make easy wear without confinement.
6. *Hooks* – use rarely. They don't stay closed with movement.
7. *Zippers* – great on short hair. Be careful not to catch hair. Also, underline a zipper with a placket that protects between dog and zipper teeth.
8. Slipovers work well on small and medium animals – even large ones.
9. Stretch fabrics, knits, jerseys and loose weaves are great for sweaters that are *pullovers*.

## DOG'S WINTER GEAR

Housedogs get acclimated to indoor temperatures. There must be a real difference to them when they go outside. In cold weather, rain, sleet or snow, a pet needs protection.

My favorite deep cold weather pet outfit comes with jacket, hat, front *legg-ons* and chaps. Dig these pictures!

## HAT

(I call this a "wind-break."). Use heavy fabric.

- Cut large square. *Measure dog's head from ear to ear across head. Add ½" all way around to allow for seam.

1. Sew. Turn comer to comer with right side in. Sew around leaving a 2" space open for turning.
2. Clip corners. This will make seams flat.
3. Turn to right side with pencil or such.
4. Gather widest side of triangle. Make this takeout about ¾" eased. The garment will cup a bit.
5. Neck strap. Use ½" wide elastic. Cut to fit snug around dog's head and neck. Stitch on both corners.
6. The cap will be a head cover that blocks wind and rain.
7. If you want the cap to stay in place when worn with coat, sew onto middle of back at bottom a 1-1/2" piece of Velcro. (Attach other part of Velcro at center neck of coat to hold into place.

Treats & Tales

## EASY SLIDE ON COAT

In the photo, the animal has a black fake fur outfit. You can buy pretty fur in fabric stores. Often for very little money you can pick up a coat at a thrift store. If so, you can cut off the sleeves for the main section of the body.

A. Cut sleeves totally out or leave about 5" of sleeve on the jacket. (You can finish sleeve bottom on jacket and make you a jacket to match).

B. Cut one sleeve length to fit your dog (measure neck to hip area).

C. Use finished cuff (if straight) for bottom. Cut other end even for your measurements. This will be the bodice.

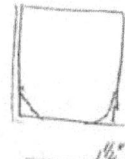

D. Cut lining fabric same size and use stretch velour for lining.

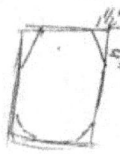

E. Place bodice and lining on top of each other. Cut corners rounded on one end for bottom. At top (neckline) cut off 1-1/2" to ease off 4" down.

F. Cut collar band out of knit (sweater, ski-knit, or stretch fabric). A smaller dog uses these measurements. Neck is 14" around plus 2" for a comfortable fit. NOTE: ALLOW ½" FOR ALL SEAMS.

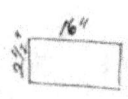

G. Belly Band. Cut this out of stretch velour. Use double layer fabric 7" one side and both 12" sides with half-inch seams.

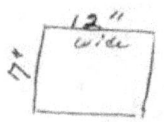

H. Make bow and center front strip by folding 1" stretch velour; unfinished sides to meet at middle then fold together. (Make about 12' of this finished cord). Stitch together.

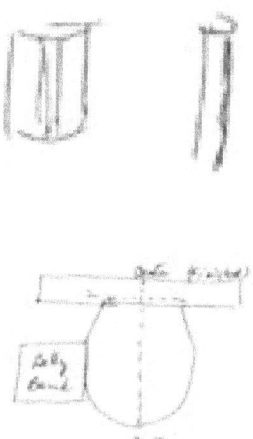

I. Now, assemble together.
   a. Find centers and sew together. (Finish the extra collar band seam by turning edge to finish).
   b. Sew belly band to one 7" side, then use Velcro on other side for closure. *This will become a tube that will open easily.
J. Place lining on bodice "right" sides together. Stitch around, but leave a small opening to turn it. (Faux fur needs a finish).

K. Top Side

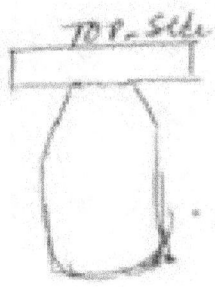

Belly-side

L. Sew neckband (collar) and close with Velcro.

M. Sew on connector (at center under neck to top side of closure). Connect to under side center by stitching.

LEGG-ONS

Easy to wear. Simple to make. Match to coat fabric.

Measure dog leg from shoulder to 3" above front ankle.

|  | Length |  | Width |
|---|---|---|---|
| Most small dogs will measure | 4" | x | 4+2" |
| Sm-medium dogs will measure | 6" | x | 8+2" |
| Medium dogs will measure | 8-10" | x | 9+2" |

The width should be 2" wider than animal's upper leg. Cut 2 pieces.

    a. Finish top and bottom edges by sewing 1/2" seam on each edge. Stitch 1/4" elastic

on "top edge." Stretch as you sew.
b. Sew together side seams.
c. Measure across animal's back from top arms
d. Cut 1" wide elastic to this measurement (plus 2 inches for finish).
e. Sew one side to the middle of one leg-tube.
f. Stitch Velcro to one side of other tube.
g. Fit by putting it on the dog. Stitch other Velcro piece for closure at the place where it snugly fits (on the elastic). Be certain to have it face other part of closure correctly.

## DOG BUNTING

This is great for small animals!
How to measure your pet:
1. Chest measure (all way around)
2. Neck
3. Neck to tail
4. Overall length
5. Length to back legs (front leg to back leg)
6. Leg height
   a. Front leg to ground
   b. Back leg to ground

Put together: Baby Dog Bunting
A. Put zipper or closure in place.
B. Sew shoulder gussets to top on each side.
C. Sew side gussets to each side top.
D. Sew shoulder gussets to underside; and sides.
E. Finish neckline, arms and legs with seam and trim edges with lace.

**BABY DRESS**

This is so easy and creates a comfortable easy garment. Buy a baby dress (thrift stores are good). The size garment will depend on the size of your animal. My Chihuahua can wear sizes 18 months to 2 years old. (A sleeved garment needs to be larger).

You can get by with fabrics that don't shred and ravel by not even sewing edges. Just cut.

1. The front of the garment will become the back.
2. Remove tags and lay flat so you are looking at the backside of garment.
3. Cut side seams open.
4. About 4 to 5 inches down from center front, cut straight to each side. (Leave sleeves in and cut beneath them). This will make a "bib" under the chin. Use existing closures for front (snaps or buttons). Otherwise sew on Velcro.
5. Set aside all extra fabrics to use for other things.
6. The front side of dress needs to be cut on each side, rounding off to the underarm. This will keep sides from dragging. (Larger and taller dogs will need less cutaway. Use your judgment. It all depends on garment and size of animal. (May not be good for a Saint Bernard!)
7. Trim to taste.

People love the fancy baby dresses. Remember to paint toenails to match.

## BASIC DOG VEST
**(Slip Over Sweater)**

These are wonderful and real simple.

1. Cut the sleeves from a sweater for fabric.
   Note: (You can make yourself a vest by hemming the sleeve holes).
2. Measure dog from between shoulders to tail.
3. Lay sweater sleeve flat on cutting table, with underarm seam toward you (this will be under side).
4. Measure:
   A. 4" down from wrist, which will be neck hole (collar point). Pin to mark.
   B. From this point, measure dog's back length and place pin there.
   C. On bottom end, add 1" and cut straight across.
   D. On bottom side (seam) measure 2 -1/2" from collar point. (Ref. A)
   E. Cut from bottom toward back of garment. (A

long split). Stop about 2-1/2" to 3" from top. Place for front feet.

F. If needed, roll hem all the way around this cut.
G. At seam on opening, stitch the two seams together with a 1/4" over-lap. This makes two leg holes for the front feet.
H. A male dog needs to have garments cut away at the underside. (For hygiene purposes).
I. Cut in quarter moon, rounding off from back top to 4" off at bottom seam.
J. Stretch and sew to make a fluted hem. (Can be left unhemmed in some fabric).

## SLIP-OVER TOBOGGAN SHIRT

Very easy and fast to make. Do several at a time. These are double-fabric, so it will be great for bad days. Good for small to medium dogs.

1. Purchase or find a toboggan hat that will work for your dog.
2. Cut hat end (the rounded top) 2" to 2-1/2" to each side of middle point. Hem a surge open seam. Trim if desired. (Be certain dogs' head will go through hole easily).
3. Make Velcro closure to tighten at neck hole.
4. Lay flat (in half); cut leg hole out. Split from bottom to 3" to 4" across toward top.
5. Finish leg hole with surger, trim or hem. This is not to be too long; shirt waist is good.

It's so easy! You can match with a toboggan for yourself. If your dog is slim, sew out any excess fabric before you trim out.

This one is geared for the person who doesn't sew. Just use your own finish ideas.

To sum it all up!

Your baby may take time to learn to wear clothes. Be patient! All the funky things like hats, pants, glasses, chaps, belts, foo-foo, and exotic will come with time.

The magic words are, "Oh look at you! You're beautiful! "

**CAT CLOTHES**

"Mousing cats" are not to be expected to wear clothes. You'll be lucky if you can talk your house pussy into being clothed.

Mostly for a feline, you can make a collar type

item that closes with Velcro or elastic. With this, you can introduce the pet to colors and fun collars.

Try a colorful turtleneck.
   a. Use a 6" band or tube of stretch knit. Cut about 8" in length. Sew ends together.
   b. Stitch ends together
   c. Gather at seam to finish about 3" if desired.
   d. For variations, you can add laces and trims.

Cats have a different personality than a dog – because they are the way they are. Cat life is a complete 100% degree turn. They are laid back if they desire or they can be frisky and outgoing. Most cats rule their house. They have a way of wrapping you around their little finger-claw until you're hooked.

Many people like cats because they train to a litter box, which is easy. They keep them indoors without struggle and don't require lots of space. Their delicate aire creates a mystic attitude that people love.

Most cats don't give a flip for a dog. They immediately put the dog on defense. A dog will chase a cat for fun and the "hunt" instinct surfaces. When the cat stops the chase, she'll be laughing from a limb of a tree and screaming for help. Sometimes, if the animals are in a small area, the cat humps the back; hair stands on end and cat screams, "I've got you now!" If the dog sticks that nose closer, cat is the aggressor and comes forth with all claws flying. Poor puppy, it hurts!

www.ingramcontent.com/pod-product-compliance
Lightning Source LLC
LaVergne TN
LVHW011934070526
838202LV00054B/4647